The Earl's Christmas Deal

A Clean Regency Romance Novel

Emily Barnet

Copyright © 2024 by Emily Barnet
All Rights Reserved.
This book may not be reproduced or transmitted in any form without the written permission of the publisher. In no way is it legal to reproduce, duplicate, or transmit any part of this document in either electronic means or in printed format. Recording of this publication is strictly prohibited and any storage of this document is not allowed unless with written permission from the publisher.

Adam Benkley
Emilia Sterling

Table of Contents

CHAPTER ONE 3
CHAPTER TWO 12
CHAPTER THREE 19
CHAPTER FOUR 26
CHAPTER FIVE 32
CHAPTER SIX 38
CHAPTER SEVEN 49
CHAPTER EIGHT 58
CHAPTER NINE 66
CHAPTER TEN 73
CHAPTER ELEVEN 83
CHAPTER TWELVE 90
CHAPTER THIRTEEN 95
CHAPTER FOURTEEN 100
CHAPTER FIFTEEN 107
CHAPTER SIXTEEN 113
CHAPTER SEVENTEEN 121
CHAPTER EIGHTEEN 126
CHAPTER NINETEEN 134
CHAPTER TWENTY 142
CHAPTER TWENTY-ONE 146
CHAPTER TWENTY-TWO 151
CHAPTER TWENTY-THREE 157
CHAPTER TWENTY-FOUR 163
CHAPTER TWENTY-FIVE 170
EPILOGUE 176
EXTENDED EPILOGUE 180

CHAPTER ONE

Long shadows danced in the firelight as Lord Adam Bentley sat hunched over his desk. His quill moved across the tenancy agreement in front of him, pausing at intervals to mark a particular passage that needed amending.

He rubbed his thumb against the quill's stem, the tip stained black with ink. Groaning, he straightened his shoulders, trying to dispel the throbbing ache in the small of his back from sitting in the same position too long. As a soft knock sounded at the door, he frowned, his thoughts scattering at the interruption.

"Enter," he called as his aunt Augusta came into the room. Adam felt the tension in his shoulders return, watching her eyes narrow as she looked about the room.

"Adam, it is near as dark as pitch in here," she said, closing the door with a flick of her wrist. The floor shuddered beneath his feet as she did so. "Why, if you can see half a foot in front of you, I would be amazed."

"I have several candles upon my desk, Aunt," Adam replied, his fingers tightening around the quill as he returned his gaze to his papers. "Granted, it may be darker by the door."

His aunt tutted under her breath, walking into the room and standing before the fire. The flames sent shimmering light across the fabric of her deep purple gown, highlighting the grey streaks in her hair. She clasped her hands in front of her and turned just enough to study him from the corner of her eye. Adam's toes curled inside his shoes as he took in her expression—it was the same one she had worn when he was a child, and he had just misbehaved.

He loved his aunt, but she was the type of woman who would not let a subject drop once she had decided it needed her attention.

He waited as she fidgeted, eventually crossing the room and taking a seat before his desk, staring at him until he looked up. Sighing, Adam lowered his quill and met her eyes.

"Yes, Aunt, how may I help you?"

"Pray, do not adopt that tone with me, my boy. You may be an earl, but I've known you since you were the height of my knee."

"Would it help if I sat cross-legged on the floor, then?" he asked. Her eyes remained narrowed, but there was a hint of a twinkle in them that had not been there before.

"I suppose you understand why I am here," she muttered.

"Indeed, I am at a loss. However, being interrupted is always a great pleasure. Reading is famously improved by the scattering of one's thoughts."

Her fingers flexed in her lap, plucking at a loose thread until she pulled it free and flicked it away across the floor.

"The Christmas season is upon us," she said as Adam's stomach rolled unpleasantly at the prospect. He cleared his throat shifting in his seat.

"Mm," he grunted.

"You need not sound quite so melancholic, Adam. It brings tidings of great joy."

"Sent by whom?" he muttered, and his aunt tutted again as she looked at the darkness that suddenly seemed to surround them.

"Will you still not permit me to add some holly to this room? The rest of the house is looking very festive."

"No. Please. No holly. I am content with my fire."

"You have a fire all year round."

"And I enjoy it immensely."

She scoffed. "Do you not think it might lift your spirits and revive your love of the holiday season if you engaged in something other than work for a change?"

Her gaze clouded as Adam's mood darkened considerably. He could not imagine anything worse than being forced to 'make merry' at this time of the year. Nothing had felt festive about Christmas for three long, tortuous years, and that was unlikely to change.

"I beg you, Aunt, I cannot have this conversation again."

"The Sternwood Christmas party is approaching," she insisted. "It would be my dearest wish that you attend this year." Augusta leaned forward in her chair, her icy blue eyes fixing him with an imploring look. "It would be an opportunity for you to engage in some activities *outside* of your office. Perhaps you will find that you can absorb the enjoyment of the season from others." She paused as the tension in his shoulder increased. "You may even find someone to your liking at such a gathering. Lady Seraphina Cheswick will be there, and she is a very fine young lady."

Adam's fist clenched against the thin stem of his quill; it gave an ominous creak, and he loosened his grip hastily. His aunt's references to his marital status were becoming a bore and far more insistent than they had once been. Not a single part of him wished to secure a wife from any quarter—and certainly not someone his aunt had decided was worthy.

"I know you hate speaking of it," Augusta continued, her voice softening as she leaned back in her chair. "Heaven knows I do not wish to upset you. But Anastasia is gone, and I hate to see you so gloomy. She loved Christmas, and she loved you. She would not wish you to spend the season in the shadows."

Adam averted her gaze, feigning interest in the documents before him, his throat tight as he pondered her request.

"Do you truly wish for the estate to pass to Frederick? That rakish fool is not worthy of a penny of your father's money."

Her words were no longer designed to evoke sympathy and concern; they were laced with real fear. Adam risked a glance up at her face, noting the heavy frown that betrayed the import of what she said.

"You will be isolated and alone for the rest of your life, my boy, and you deserve to be happy."

"Alright!" he snapped, and at her flinch, he lowered his voice and sighed. "Alright," he repeated more quietly. "I will attend the damned party. Will that do?"

His aunt beamed at him, rising from her chair and walking around the large desk to kiss the top of his head.

"Yes. That will do. You know how grateful I am, and it may not be as terrible as you might assume."

"You are filling me with confidence."

She paused her head on one side, staring at the door. "Could I perhaps add a sprig of mistletoe above the threshold?"

"I shall cast it into the fire should you do so," he replied, a fleeting smirk tugging at the corners of his mouth.

She sighed and squeezed her fingers around his shoulder. "Light some more candles then. You will go blind before you are five and thirty at this rate."

She kissed the top of his head once more, a little longer than before, as her hand lingered on his shoulder in an affectionate gesture of support, and then she left him to the gloom.

Adam watched her go, his head beginning to pound with a headache.

Leaning back in his chair, he stared into the flames of the fire, contemplating all she had said, a familiar numbness creeping through his muscles at the prospect of yet another Christmas without his family.

His fingers involuntarily twitched toward the top drawer of his desk, and after a few thoughtful moments, he opened it and drew out the picture of his mother. Her face stared back at him from the gilded frame, more radiant every time he held it. Adam gently ran a finger over it, his thoughts scattering again; his mind filled with Anastasia.

By the time he had thought to have a portrait of his late wife painted it was far too late. The disease that had finally claimed her had stripped all the life and colour from her cheeks. He remembered her as vividly now as ever, but the large portrait in the gallery did not do her justice. He wished he could have commissioned another version of her, one he could have kept with him always.

Rubbing a hand over his forehead, he rose from his chair and stretched. His back clicked violently as he glanced at the clock. He had been working for five hours without a pause, and his body ached damnably.

Standing beside his desk, he was motionless for a few minutes, his gaze fixed on his mother's face. The late Countess of Bellebrook had been a sensible, gentle-hearted woman who doted on him. The memory of her final days still caused a desperate jolt of pain in his chest, and he took a deep breath to banish it.

Even speaking of consumption made him shudder. Any time it was brought up in conversation, he would excuse himself or attempt to rapidly change the subject. He supposed, in some ways, he should be grateful. His mother had been spared the agonies many experienced with that disease, but to him, at just sixteen, he sometimes wondered if he would have preferred a longer farewell.

One morning, the hacking cough she had experienced rattled through the house with morbid regularity. Then, when he had gone in to visit her that afternoon, she was gone. It had broken his heart, and the blasted holly about her bed had forever bound his hatred for the Christmas season ever since.

And then, blissfully, Anastasia had revived it.

Her enthusiasm for all things festive was unquenchable and, ultimately, impossible to ignore. His love for his wife had driven away the sadness he had felt every time Christmas came around each year, and she began to instil in him new happiness. Their whirlwind courtship had been a joyful, magical time during which the burdens of his life had been cast aside in place of love.

At Christmas, they always sang carols at the piano in Bellebrook Manor, his baritone mixing with her soprano, her laughter echoing through the corridors like a beautiful bell.

But then her voice had faded.

The lung fever that had taken hold of her after only three years of marriage had been rampant and vicious. Adam had grown to hate it more than anything else in his life.

He had been determined to save Anastasia, refusing to watch another woman he loved fade away without a fight. He had spoken to over thirty doctors in the course of the following year. They had tried everything to help her—bleeding, poultices, leeches—and every tonic imaginable.

Some remedies had even seemed to work for a little while, but Anastasia grew steadily weaker and had been bedridden for the final few months of her life. Adam now regretted the madness that had taken hold of him. He had travelled the country to find a cure, taking him away from Anastasia when he should have been at her side.

Only when their physician finally told him the grave truth did he realise the dreadful reality of all that he had wasted and the life he had lost. He had held her hand from that day onwards, and she had clung on for another two months before that dreadful rattling breathing had finally faded entirely.

Her death had almost broken him again, a horrible mixture of the pain of his mother's passing now inextricably mixed with Anastasia's too. Only his estate and his work had saved him, and he was disinclined to change that when he brought him such comfort.

He rarely left his office before the evening, and when he wasn't travelling to see his tenants, he would be at his desk before the lark.

Adam poked at the fire, noting the ink stains all over his hands—he would have to wash before supper. He returned the poker to the stand, holding out his hands before him and examining them. They seemed suddenly old in the firelight, withered by grief, as though he were an elderly man himself. But then he looked again, and they had returned to normal. At two and thirty, he should hardly have felt as late on in years as he did.

Adam rubbed his hand over his face again, angry with himself for allowing his aunt to strongarm him into attending the Sternwood party. She would undoubtedly throw him at every eligible woman available and embarrass him horribly.

Adam grunted irritably and headed to his room to clean the ink from his fingers. He was hungry and out of sorts—perhaps some food and a change in company might improve that a little.

***

After supper, Adam sat in his study with his cousin, Lord Lionel Spencer.

Lionel was every bit the gentleman Adam was not. Although they shared the same blue-green eyes and chiselled features, Lionel was all affable positivity, while Adam was melancholy and withdrawn. His maternal cousin exuded warmth from every pore and was incredibly kind. He had been a steady force for good in Adam's life and Adam was grateful to call him his closest friend.

They sat before the fire in Adam's study, Lionel having arrived for supper and remained long into the night as was his wont.

Adam glanced at him over the rim of his brandy glass. Lionel was looking particularly handsome these days. He was five years younger than Adam, but they had been thick as thieves since they were children. His longer-than-fashionable dark hair was swept back from his face, high cheekbones reflecting the firelight.

Adam returned his gaze to the fire as Lionel yawned widely and stretched his long legs out toward the flames.

"What vexes you so?" his cousin asked, his head on one side, eyebrows raised in query.

"Mm?" Adam asked, feigning ignorance, though he knew he had been silent at dinner, and both his aunt and cousin had commented upon it.

"Come now, you are not always the most gregarious, but I have not heard you speak two words tonight. What is it? The Christmas soiree cannot be all bad. At least you do not have to host the thing; that would be far more onerous." Adam didn't reply, and his cousin looked over at him with concern. "What is it, dear cousin? You are not yourself."

"Your mother wants me to remarry," he said, feeling the bile rise in his throat at the thought. "She has not stopped speaking of it for several weeks." Lionel remained silent, for which Adam was grateful. "I cannot even conceive of it. Anastasia may have been gone for many years, but her loss is still raw. I do not know if I could entertain thoughts of another, let alone be thrust among several eligible ladies at the party."

"But these are my mother's wishes, Bentley, not yours. You do not have to do anything you are not comfortable with."

"I know, but a part of me is also aware that she is right. She has fears of the line passing to Frederick."

Lionel grimaced. "Heaven help us all."

Adam chuckled. "Exactly. If I do not remarry, I will never secure an heir, and a future where Frederick inherits is certain. But I cannot imagine opening my heart again. The loss of losing someone you love—it haunts me still."

"Of course it does," Lionel said softly with unending patience. "I have not lost anyone close to me, and for that, I am truly grateful. No one who has not lived it can understand it, and you cannot drag yourself out of grief for your aunt's benefit."

Adam stared into the flames, swirling the liquid in his glass and trying to gather his thoughts.

"I do sometimes wonder if it is of my choosing," he muttered, finally voicing the worry that had plagued him for several months.

"What do you mean by that?" Lionel asked, sitting up a little in his chair.

"It is easy to work, to remain hidden from the world. The festive season holds no joy for me, and it is simpler to continue to hate it than try to love it." Adam shook his head. "Sometimes it feels as though my mind is steering me down a darker path deliberately. That the darkness is more inviting somehow—easier to be in the shadow than face the light."

"And if it is?"

Adam looked at him, Lionel's face was all concern. "You do not think I should fight against the feeling?"

Lionel looked back into the flames, his lips thinning as they compressed together. He took a long sip of his brandy and rested it gently against his knee.

"I would not presume to advise either way. You have seen much pain in your life and have lost a great deal. To guard your heart is ingrained within you, and that is not to be criticised." Lionel placed his glass on the table between them and leaned forward, fixing Adam with a gentle stare. "But all I will say is that you are your own person. You are free to choose what suits *your* life, not your aunt's, not your future fortune. You."

Adam watched his friend's earnest gaze become more resolute.

"What you say is true," Lionel continued. "Pulling oneself out of melancholy takes effort, but you must do it at your own pace. I grant you that the party will be dripping with Christmas cheer, and your damnably handsome face will have the ladies swooning all about the place," Adam scoffed derisively, "but it *will* be a chance to allow external influence to move you. Other people's joy—other people's company—can be a great help when one is downcast. Nothing is certain except that if you remain in your study throughout the season, nothing with change."

Adam felt warmth spread through his chest at his cousin's sentiment. Lionel was not advising him so much as reassuring him. It was a relief, having only had his aunt's derisive and commanding comments over the past few weeks.

"Thank you," Adam said. "You are right, of course. And *you* will be at the party. If it is unbearable, I can spend my time beating you at billiards."

"Hah! Fat chance of that," Lionel said good-naturedly and then rose, bowing low to the ground and making Adam laugh before he bid him goodnight.

Adam took his time finishing his own brandy and went up to bed, a little lighter in step than he had been earlier that evening. Villiers, his loyal and meticulous valet, nodded in greeting as Adam entered his bed chamber and set about assisting him to undress. The man was quiet and polite but did not speak over much, which Adam appreciated.

His mind was still a mess of conflicting emotions as he climbed into bed. He was uncertain about what was going to happen, and that in itself was unusual. He had organised his life around routine, ensuring that he always knew what the day would bring. The Sternwood party meant uncertainty and unpredictability, and that could spell disaster.

As he sank into the depths of sleep, Anastasia's face swam before him, vivid, loving, and hauntingly beautiful. She was surrounded by the warm glow of Christmas candlelight, a familiar joy in her eyes. He reached for her, looking forward to holding her in his arms again, but as soon as their fingers touched, he awoke with a start.

The night around him was dark and cold, a flurry of snow pattering against the windowpane. His aunt had placed some holly on the mantelpiece above the fire in his room with a tartan ribbon below it, and he scowled at it angrily.

Grief warred with anticipation in his chest. Despite himself, he could not shake the feeling that the party spelled the beginning of something new. No matter how much he dreaded the prospect, it felt like the tides were shifting toward a different future, but it was unclear whether it would be for good or ill.

CHAPTER TWO

Many miles away in Sternwood Manor, Lady Emilia Sterling was lost in Bach's Concerto in D Minor.

The sun streamed in through the windows beside her, warming her face. It should have lifted her spirits, but she was mired in the past, the music only serving as another reminder of all she had lost.

Her fingers moved dexterously over the keys of the pianoforte, her eyes closed, her mind shut off from the world around her. The piece was sombre and slow, perfectly suiting her mood.

As it swelled to its crescendo, she felt her right hand falter as her index finger slipped from the keys, and she was catapulted back to two years before. Her jaw clenched at the memory as she returned to the beauty of Countess Blackmoor's drawing room.

Seats were arranged before the piano, waiting for the concert to come, and Emilia felt the familiar buzz of excitement skittering beneath her skin as she waited for her turn. There was nothing in her life that she loved so much as performing.

The concert had been one of her greatest triumphs, her performance faultless. She had received acclaim from many high-ranking members of the Ton, and as she left the piano, the son of her host, Lord Julian Blackmoor, approached her to praise her accomplishments.

They had enjoyed a lively discussion about the music, and it was wonderful to talk with another enthusiast about her love of the complex arrangement she had mastered and to receive the same passion in return.

But it wasn't long before she realised, in the excitement of the moment, that she had forgotten her decorum, leaning into Lord Julian as they innocently extolled the wonders of Mozart. When she looked up, she saw Henrietta Darcy watching them with narrowed eyes. Emilia quickly leaned away from Lord Julian and ended the conversation, but the damage was already done.

Fiercely jealous of Emilia's abilities, Henrietta was her greatest rival. She had jumped at the chance to ruin Emilia on the world stage.

The following day, parlours all over London were rife with rumours that Emilia Sternwood was using her charm to corrupt a married man.

Despite Lord Julian and Countess Blackmoor vehemently denying the rumours, it did no good. The invitations Emilia had grown accustomed to receiving, inviting her to perform at the houses of their acquaintances, dried up almost overnight.

The humiliation of the affair had been hard enough for Emilia to cope with, but it was her parents who were most affected by it. As an only child, her musical talents and accomplishments had been a source of great pride to Lord and Lady Sternwood.

It had been Emilia's greatest shame to watch her parents' hopes for her fade into nothing. At first, they staunchly defended her to anyone who might suggest impropriety. Still, as the rumours grew wider and more vicious over time, the acceptance and support she had felt initially began to wane in the face of public disapproval.

It was soon apparent that any hope of salvaging her reputation had been dashed to pieces.

Emilia abruptly stopped playing. Looking outside into the sun, she felt the burn against her eyes as she tried to regain her composure.

Her fingers lifted from the keys as she took a deep breath, looking out at the frost-bitten gardens before her. The ice was thick upon the ground, and stalactites had formed overnight in sparkling points at the base of the bird bath in front of the window.

Emilia jolted violently as the door to the drawing room opened, and her mother entered. Lady Camilla Sterling swept into the room, careless of interrupting her daughter's practice. She was followed by Catherine, their overeager maid, who carried a large tray laden with tea and cake before her.

Her mother did not apologise to Emilia or even glance in her direction. Emilia's stomach clenched as her mother sat on the settee, patiently waiting for her daughter to join her, not saying a word.

Catherine bustled about laying the tea down for them and settling a plate of small cakes in the centre before hurrying out. Emilia dutifully rose and made her way to sit opposite her mother.

"That was rather mournful," her mother said as she poured her a cup. "I prefer it when you play more cheerful pieces."

Emilia bit her tongue and forced a smile. "I shall play something like that tomorrow then."

They sat in awkward silence for a few more minutes, Emilia longing for the time when she and her mother spoke for hours on a variety of subjects without pausing for breath, but those days were gone.

Lady Sternwood had always claimed that she understood her daughter's predicament, that in her heart, she knew Emilia had done nothing wrong. But Emilia still felt that her mother blamed her for the position the Sternwood family now held in society. They were no longer of the elite class they had once enjoyed.

"The Christmas party is approaching us," her mother said suddenly, lowering her teacup to her saucer and spearing Emilia with a long stare. Her brown eyes were dark and heavy against her copper-coloured hair.

"Yes, Mama, I am looking forward to it," she lied.

"Your father is most eager that you make the acquaintance of the Duke of Elderbridge. He is a revered gentleman and has met your father several times. He is quite willing to overlook the scandal with the Blackmoors and has recently rejoined the marriage mart after the loss of his wife."

Emilia's fingers tightened around the handle of her teacup, sipping it carefully. She had learned long ago that speaking her mind too quickly generally got her into trouble. The idea of marrying Benedict Easton, the Duke of Elderbridge, repulsed her. He was twice her age—more so at forty-eight—and had six daughters fully grown. She could well imagine why he wished for a wife—he would want a son.

Emilia nodded as she noticed her mother waiting for a response.

"I see," she said cautiously, "have you met him, Mama?"

"I have not, but I trust your father implicitly. He would not recommend someone he did not believe worthy."

Worthy of a woman who has been disgraced and cannot expect anything better, Emilia thought bitterly.

She loved her parents, but her relationship with them had changed beyond recognition since the scandal. They were both hesitant to allow her any freedom and did not seem to notice that their continual references to their daughter's limited options in society caused her daily pain.

She longed to play in a room full of people again, but that time was also over. She would have to content herself with playing melancholy pieces in the privacy of her own home.

As she considered that bleak prospect, the door to the drawing room opened again, and their butler entered, bowing to the room.

"My Lady, the Fairfaxes have arrived," he said stiffly, and behind him, Catherine entered again with another tray of tea for their guests.

Emilia's heart rejoiced as Lord and Lady Fairfax entered, followed by their daughter Charlotte. The two younger women had been best friends since childhood, and her presence was a balm to Emilia's soul. As Charlotte entered, she gave Emilia a meaningful look and it was clear there was much for them to discuss once their parents had begun conversing.

The Fairfaxes all sat down. Elizabeth Fairfax was the same age as Camilla Sterling, and the two women were similar in beliefs and temperament. Charlotte and Emilia had grown to be experts at navigating their mother's changeable wills.

Emilia's father soon joined them, and he and Lord Fairfax quickly began to speak of the gelding that the latter had recently purchased. Emilia's mother launched into a tirade to Lady Fairfax about the stresses of hosting a Christmas party and how preparations were progressing. Indeed, Emilia had never seen so much ribbon as had been delivered to the manor in recent weeks. Her mother was determined to show that she was capable of throwing the best Christmas event of the season.

Charlotte sat opposite Emilia, the unspoken conversation between them palpable as Emilia's mother moved on to the *excellent* Duke of Elderbridge and all the wonderful things he had accomplished in his life. After enduring this for a further ten minutes, Charlotte dutifully mentioned that she longed for some fresh air and she and Emilia escaped before their mothers found someone that Charlotte could be married off to, as well.

As they closed the outer door behind them, Emilia gave a sigh of relief. Her breath formed in great clouds about her. It was brutally cold, and she was grateful for her muff and hat.

The day was crisp, and the sky was heavy with the promise of snow. The edges of the lawns were lined with fir trees hanging low to the ground, and the women walked along the paths arm in arm, their feet crunching over the crisp ground in unison.

Emilia made it a reasonable distance from the house before she stamped her foot and scoffed so loudly that she startled a robin pecking at the earth nearby.

"The Duke of *Elderbridge*," she spat as Charlotte's arm tightened around hers. "I declare he is over twenty-five years older than me, with *six* daughters, three of whom are unmarried and must be younger than I am! Apparently, this is all I can expect from the world of suitors now. The cast-offs of widows who are willing to *overlook* a scandal that did not even happen." She kicked a stone viciously along the path as they walked, her nose almost numb already from the bitter cold.

"I cannot believe they are considering him," Charlotte replied with cold fury.

"Why would they not consider him? I have no other prospects. I cannot set foot in any hallway or drawing room in the country without someone wondering if I will steal their husband!"

"Emilia," Charlotte said with a long-suffering sigh, "that is simply not true. You are highly regarded amongst our close acquaintances and everybody knows you did nothing wrong. I blame the countess for her dismissal of you. It was badly done. She has not even tried to visit you."

"If she were to visit me, it would only intensify the rumours," Emilia retorted. "And to think I once had one and twenty suitors willing to dance with me and five invitations a week for private concerts. Now, if I were invited to a funeral, I would be surprised."

Charlotte snorted loudly, and Emilia glanced at her friend to see her smiling reproachfully. Her good humour was contagious, however, and they both began to laugh. Despite her simmering anger, Emilia's mood lifted at Charlotte's presence.

"If I were to die, I would ensure you were invited to my funeral," Charlotte said reassuringly.

"I am so grateful, Charlotte, thank you. But if you were to die, I would insist that you haunt me so I have someone to keep me company." Charlotte's tinkling laugh carried over the air. "And as I understand it, the estimable *Miss Henrietta Darcy* is the bell of the ball these days.".

Charlotte scowled. "She was at a recital I attended recently and had the audacity to come and speak to me."

"Charlotte, my love, I would never expect you to reject her entirely purely on my account."

"Oh, it is not only on your account, I assure you. She is a vicious creature. I cannot abide being in the same room with her for more than five minutes. She speaks of herself in the third person and uses the royal 'we' whenever she refers to her practice of the piano. Vile thing."

Emilia squeezed her friend's arm, feeling a rush of affection for her. Charlotte rarely spoke of the scandal unless Emilia brought it up herself, and it was refreshing to hear her so furious about it nearly two years later.

"But I would not lose hope," Charlotte continued. "The duke may be eligible, to be sure, but there will be other men at the Christmas ball who might be to your liking. Nothing is certain, and it has been a long time since the rumours began. Your family is hosting this event, and your mother will largely control what will take place. There can be no expectation for fresh scandal, and you will be able to play before the company for the first time in months. Focus on that if nothing else. I have longed to hear you play for months."

"You are right," Emilia replied with a sigh. "I am sorry Charlotte, I am being very petulant today. I suppose it is a fresh wound upon a wound to learn that I am on the shelf already."

"None of that. You, my dear, are the most beautiful woman in the world," Charlotte declared, her voice firm yet soft."

"This is why I adore you," Emilia said warmly. "You always lift my spirits."

"It is my duty, after all. I will not see you so downcast. Have you spoken to your mother of your reticence about the Duke?"

Emilia sighed heavily. "It would be quite hopeless. All my parents think about now is how they will marry me off. I do not fault them; I am well aware that my isolation has weighed heavily upon them both, but Mama would not understand. To her, an eligible marriage bears far more importance than my own sentiments.; she has made that abundantly clear."

"Well, It pains me to hear it," Charlotte stated wearily, "yet, in her fashion, she *does* care for you."

"She does. But any closeness there once was between us has slowly degraded over time. If I were to broach the subject, it would be yet another argument at the end of an already tumultuous year. It would get us nowhere."

"Then let us not lose hope that the duke may meet you and be utterly repulsed by your haggard appearance."

Emilia laughed loudly, and Charlotte grinned. They continued on beneath the weak winter sunshine, walking past the frozen pond and crisp, silent grasses immobilised by frost.

However, Emilia's smile slowly faded as she considered the upcoming party. She usually loved Christmas; it had once been her favourite time of year, but it felt tarnished somehow. The shine very much dimmed, even as the house became more and more festive around her.

Perhaps she *would* find someone to her liking at the party. Yet, there remained the troubling question of whether he would be able to look beyond the shadows cast by her past. No one in society was ignorant of the rumours that clung to her—unfounded though they were—and the more one endeavoured to refute such talk, the more it seemed to mark one as a liar.

It was a cruel truth, but the fact that a widower wanted to wed her was an unpleasant sign of what was to come. Only a desperate man would want her.

It had been two years, and yet sometimes, it felt like her disgrace had only happened yesterday. She looked up at the white sky, the clouds heavy with snow, and prayed that this Christmas, her fortunes might change.

She squeezed Charlotte's arm and felt an answering tightening against her own.

My future may hang in the balance over the coming days, but at least I am not alone.

CHAPTER THREE

A week later, Emilia stood at the top of the grand staircase, her heart heavy with trepidation as she watched the carriages approach. Sternwood Manor was unrecognisable after her mother's attentions over the last week, and she had to admit, it looked wonderful.

Practically every surface was adorned with greenery. Ivy and laurel wreaths hung above many of the doorways, and evergreen branches from the gardens were laid across each mantelpiece. The stairs themselves were hung with silver and gold ornaments that sparkled in the candlelight, and Emilia found herself enjoying the sight of them for the first time in many years.

There seemed to be an atmosphere of hope in the house. She had rejoiced in it at first until she realised the cause. Her mother's good mood, and therefore her father's, was due to their expectations of the duke and his imminent arrival.

Emilia swallowed as she glanced down the long flight of stairs, trying to get a handle on her nerves. It was the first event of this kind she had attended since the scandal. Even though her parents were the hosts, she still felt on edge and vulnerable in high society again.

Descending the stairs, she joined her mother and father at the doorway, greeting the guests as they entered. Everyone seemed polite and friendly as they passed her, but many in society were adept at hiding their true feelings until they were in private.

The crunch of gravel outside caught her attention, and a magnificent carriage arrived, pulled by a team of four black stallions. Her mother stiffened instantly, and a wave of nausea rushed through Emilia's body as she recognised who it must be.

Rich as Croesus, she thought irritably, *that'll please Mother.*

From the carriage stepped a tall man with greying, dark brown hair. He had a neat beard clipped close to his chin and bright green eyes that peered up at the house with interest. His lips were thin; his face pinched as though he were evaluating everything in his path. Emilia disliked the look of him immediately.

Behind him, three women emerged from the carriage. They were about the same height and perhaps two or three years older than each other. Emilia was reminded of the sisters in King Lear and tried to work out which two were Goneril and Regan.

They had dark hair like their father, were impeccably dressed in the latest fashions, and had a sneering, unpleasant countenance as though their father's judgments had passed directly onto them.

Emilia had never felt such a profound dislike for so many people on sight before, but her father strode forward promptly as the duke ascended the steps and shook his hand.

All of the daughters wore polite smiles now, but their eyes were cold. In perfect unison, they turned to regard Emilia, as though their movements had been choreographed in advance. Their identical brown eyes looked her up and down as one being—it was the most critical appraisal she had ever been subjected to.

Sophia, Penelope, and Caroline Easton. They were a formidable sight. Sophia was the eldest and gave Emilia such an icy glare that she was surprised she was not frozen to the spot. The two younger girls turned to one another to whisper and burst into giggles, receiving a firm glare from their father.

I may become their stepmother in time. Emilia thought hopelessly. *What a terrible fate to have thrust upon me.*

She stiffened as the duke approached her, a slight smile on his face as his eyes ran over her body in a way that made her skin crawl.

"Lady Emilia," he said dutifully, bowing to her as her mother watched their interaction eagerly. "It is a pleasure to make your acquaintance."

He pressed a kiss to her hand, and Emilia compelled herself to relax as he straightened.

"Likewise, your Grace," she said formally, retracting her hand as soon as she was able and plucking at the edge of her dress as the duke bowed to her parents and made his way into the ballroom. His three daughters followed behind, gliding into the room with an effortless grace Emilia could never hope to achieve.

Emilia could just imagine her future at Elderbridge House, sitting silently amidst her inherited family. She envisioned herself seated at a long dining table, her sole companions her icy husband and his even colder daughters. Perhaps once she had given him the heir he craved, she might spend all her time alone or locked in a bedroom in the tallest tower, waiting for her knight to come and rescue her.

As Emilia was considering her future and the dim prospects before her, another carriage drew up to the manor. In it, Adam sat with his aunt and Lionel. He watched the house slowly grow larger out of the window and was wracked by a deep sense of uncertainty. Nerves rumbled unpleasantly in his gut, and he could feel his palms sweating inside his evening gloves.

Whyever did I agree to this? Two weeks trapped in a house with a group of strangers. I would rather fall through the surface of a frozen river.

"I am so pleased the Sternwoods are holding their party again this year," his aunt proclaimed happily.

"Why would they not?" Lionel asked, and his mother rolled her eyes dramatically.

"You know of the rumours, Lionel. I have told you a hundred times."

"I am sorry, Mother, but I do not hold with gossip."

Adam turned to his aunt with a frown. "You cannot mean what was said about Lord Julian Blackmoor?"

"Of course I mean it! There were many pernicious comments at the time, and the Sternwoods have not held this event since. I had thought they might recoil from society altogether, but I am glad they have not. I have always liked Camilla Sternwood. She is terribly sensible."

"Didn't the countess herself deny the rumours?" Adam asked. He hated any type of gossip and remembered there had been no *evidence* of any impropriety, only hearsay.

"She did. I have never believed Lady Emilia capable of what she was accused of. Her mother is adamant that nothing took place, and that is good enough for me."

Adam breathed a sigh of relief as the carriage drew to a halt. The last thing he needed whilst they were in the company of their hostess was his aunt making jibes about the Sterlings' conduct. He loved his aunt a great deal, but her tongue could cut glass.

They all descended from the carriage, Lionel helping his mother down as they looked up at the house. It was a fine building, pale and ornate, with pillars at the front and a beautiful swathe of ivy climbing one side, its evergreen foliage lending a sense of life to the barrenness of winter.

Adam looked about him at the milling guests arriving, feeling very out of place. He was not accustomed to society these days and disliked the idea that he could not escape over the coming days.

They ascended the stairs and Adam winced as his aunt gave a shrill shriek of delight as she saw Camilla Sternwood, a beautiful lady standing beside her husband in the main entrance hall. The two women embraced, and as they did so, they revealed a graceful young woman standing behind her parents. She had long chestnut hair and large hazel-green eyes framed by long lashes.

She was extremely beautiful but stood back from her parents as though to fade into the shadows. Adam felt a jolt of sympathy for her and wished he could do the same.

Then Emilia looked up at him, and Adam found it difficult to catch his breath.

It was as though he were looking at a mirror image of his own pain and grief. There was a darkness at the back of her eyes, a hidden sorrow as though offering a permanent apology to the world. It was as if an unspoken conversation occurred between them in those few seconds, a recognition he could not name but burned so brightly it quite overwhelmed him.

"You are staring, cousin," Lionel said discreetly, leaning against him and breaking the spell.

Mortified, Adam returned his attention to his hosts, shaking hands with Lord Sternwood and trying not to look at his daughter again. It was more difficult than it should have been.

What an idiotic introduction, he thought irritably. *Two steps inside the house, and I have already disgraced myself.*

He hurried after his aunt and cousin, keeping his back straight, his gait steady, trying to ensure that no one could pick up on the disquiet swirling in his mind.

As the final guests were shown to their rooms, Emilia breathed a sigh of relief at the sudden silence that fell upon the house. She considered the prelude to the evening ball a success. She had only detected derision and disdain from the Duke of Elderbridge's daughters. Few other attendees appeared concerned by her presence.

Checking behind her to ensure her mother was not monitoring her every move, she walked along the corridor and into the drawing room. It was blissfully empty, and she quickly made her way to the pianoforte, running her fingers over the keys and knowing that nothing else in the world would calm her as effectively as creating the music she loved.

She sat down before the piano and began to play a piece by Bach from memory. It was a spritely tune that she knew her mother would approve of with a house so full of guests. She wondered about playing something more festive, but the keys called to her of their own accord, and soon she was lost in the lilting melody.

Her mind moved to the duke and his daughters against her will. The thought of becoming their stepmother was a terrifying prospect. She could picture years stretching before her with nothing but empty halls and anger for company. His daughters regarded her as a figure of fun, someone neither to be feared nor obeyed. She knew that if she were to act as their stepmother, they would never view her as anything other than a pawn in their father's ambition to have a son.

That was how she had felt when the duke met her gaze. His eyes had been assessing and calculating—she had felt like a prize piece of meat he had come to buy. It made her feel faintly ill.

She much preferred the blue-green gaze of the Earl of Bellebrook. Emilia opened her eyes at the surprising thought and cocked her head to one side, thinking through their interaction.

Perhaps *attention* was not the correct term, but there had been something deeply intense about the way the earl had looked at her. It was almost as though he had seen into her soul, observing the person and not the scandal. It had been exhilarating.

He is also impossibly handsome, a voice in her mind said unhelpfully.

Indeed, the earl was by far the most attractive man in the company and there was a hardness and intensity about him that stirred something within her. She tried to shake off the unusual feelings and the clenching of her gut as she remembered his dark gaze. She continued to play—throwing her full attention into the music once more.

Above the drawing room, where the piano's music faded to almost nothing, many corridors twined behind rooms and through passageways as servants scurried about, seeing to the whims of their guests.

In one of the bed chambers, Adam paced before the fire, hoping to shake the tightness in his chest.

He felt as though the walls were closing in around him. Now alone, and without the company of his aunt and cousin, he was on edge, his skin crawling with the need to get outside into the open. He felt trapped in the house already and had not even managed an hour within its walls.

He ran a hand through his hair, tugging at the strands and trying to get his mind to settle before he disgraced himself. The dinner bell had not yet chimed; indeed, he was not even dressed appropriately, but he longed to feel the breeze on his face and look up at the wide sky.

Somehow, going outside felt far more appealing than remaining in his room. Aware that his aimless wandering might be met with disapproval, Adam resolved to be quick about it, hoping his hosts would not take undue offence.

Catching a glimpse of himself in the mirror above the fireplace, he straightened his cravat and ensured he was presentable before leaving his room as swiftly as possible. Perhaps he would find an unlocked door where he could escape, hiding in the gardens for a good while and enjoying the sun's pale glow on his face.

The corridors outside his bedroom were adorned with beautiful tartan bows on every picture he passed. The house smelled of cinnamon and brandy, and he sucked in a lungful of air, a strange nostalgia and sadness mixing within him as, at first, he rejoiced at the scent before quashing the feeling at the memory of Anastasia.

He had made his way to the ground floor without being detected by anyone. He was relieved to find a cold draft of air coming from somewhere, which suggested a door had been left ajar, and his hopes for escape were a little more certain.

He followed the chill that crept against his skin, and as he turned a corner into a narrow corridor, his feet came to a halt without conscious thought.

Someone was playing a beautiful piece of music and the sound of it floated towards him, hauntingly familiar and evocative.

He breathed shallowly as he recognised the strains of Bach's Little Fugue in G Minor. His mother had loved that piece. It instantly reminded him of her, her happy smile and bright, sparkling eyes leaping to the front of his mind as though it were his mother herself who was playing, conjured by the spirit of the season.

He was moving before he realised where he was headed, following the sound as a fox follows the scent of a hare, his escape forgotten, a new veracious need to find the player embedded within his mind.

He found himself in a wide corridor with high white doors all along it. One of them was partially open, and he made for it, knowing instinctively that the music must be coming from there.

He tiptoed to the crack in the door, aware that he was prying into a world he had not been invited to. Powerless in the moment, he could not help but move closer, and what he saw was an image that would stay with him forever.

Lady Emilia Sterling was the sole occupant of the room, seated at the pianoforte, her fingers fluttering over the keys as if they moved of their own accord. Her eyes were closed, her face softened in rapture as the music swelled and ebbed, ascending in glorious harmonics that filled the air with raw emotion.

But it was no longer simply the music that captivated Adam; it was the expression on the lady's face. Her eyes remained closed, no sheet music to guide her—she was playing entirely from memory, utterly enraptured by the piece. Her body swayed with each crescendo, her fingers pressing the keys with such natural grace that it seemed as though the music had become an extension of her very soul. Every part of her was absorbed, as though she were wrapped in the tight, rich column of sound she alone had conjured into existence.

The passion in the room was almost tangible, saturating the air with an intensity that struck him to his core. At that moment, something inside Adam broke free—an unbridled flood of joy and longing that he had long thought locked away, perhaps forever. His heart raced in his chest, filling with a warmth he had not felt since before Anastasia's death.

It was as if the music had somehow given voice to his own tangled emotions, loosening the knot of grief he had carried all these years. His chest expanded, his shoulders softened, and his fingers gripped the edge of the door to steady himself, unable to look away from the vision before him. He was wholly, irrevocably transfixed, as though every forgotten feeling within him was being awakened by the beauty she summoned one delicate note at a time.

CHAPTER FOUR

Emilia was lost in thought as she played.

Her mind was still musing on the earl's intentions and what he might have meant by looking at her in such a way. As the piece continued to flow through her, she opened her eyes, only for them to alight on the same blue-green gaze watching her from a crack in the door.

Her heart lurched into her throat—could he tell the subject of her thoughts by sight alone?

Her fingers froze on the keys, the final note reverberating between them like a ripple across a divide. Their eyes locked and held once more, and that strange force rose between them again. The air crackled with unspoken words, and in his eyes, she thought she discerned an echo of her own rapture, her own wonder at the love and joy music could bring.

Then, as though awoken by the pause in the music, the earl blinked, his face flushing slightly. She heard him clear his throat, and then he spun on his heel and away, leaving her wondering what had compelled him to watch her in such a manner and why she felt bereft at his absence.

Adam only noticed he was running when he skidded to a halt in the expansive foyer by the entrance of the house, startling a servant who looked up at him in surprise. He slowed his pace to a more leisurely speed and tried to quiet his mind from the whirlwind of thoughts that were bouncing around inside it.

I barely know the woman; how can she have such an effect on me purely through music?

It had been years since he had felt joy at that sound. His mother and Anastasia had both loved the piano and played it often, but *nothing* like that. Even his mother's playing was not as exquisite as what he had just heard. He swallowed convulsively around the lump in his throat and was just about to head outside when someone called his name.

Lionel approached his cousin as quickly as he could, having seen him sprint past the room he was in, looking pale and upset.

In the carriage that afternoon, Lionel had watched Adam's face growing paler and paler as they reached the house, and now he found him almost sprinting out of the door as though he might run all the way back to London.

"Bentley, old chap, whatever is the matter?" Lionel asked lightly, coming up behind him and attempting a cheerful tone. Close up, Adam looked even more discomfited, and Lionel placed a hand on his shoulder, feeling deep concern for him. "What is it, cousin, are you quite well?"

Adam closed his eyes in despair.

"I was about to take a turn in the grounds," Adam said stiffly. Lionel looked past him at the frost on every surface. He hated the winter months, disliked being cold, and had no time for snow and ice. He preferred the balmy spring days and warmth of autumn to the white wonderland that faced him now.

"Excellent, I was just about to do the same," he said swiftly, the lie rolling off his tongue effortlessly. Summoning a servant, Lionel placed a hand on Adam's arm in an attempt to forestall his swift escape.

Once wrapped up against the cold, they both walked slowly out of the door and into the wide grounds of the house.

Frost adorned every stem and flower before them, and cobwebs cascaded from every tree, catching the early evening light as the day surrendered to twilight.

Lionel kept quiet, admiring the scenery. He might hate the winter, but he would admit it had a beautiful charm about it when one paid close attention. He kept stoically silent, waiting for Adam to speak. He knew his friend was not accustomed to a party such as this. Indeed, Lionel had admonished his mother for insisting his cousin attend it at all, but she had been adamant that Adam just needed to get out, and then all would be well.

Looking at his cousin's pale and worried face, it seemed his mother had made a grave error.

"What is it?" he said finally. Adam was wringing his hands together repeatedly and hadn't uttered a word for many minutes. Neither of them had thought to bring gloves, and their fingers were pink and swollen in the freezing air.

"You will think me very foolish," Adam muttered.

"I can promise you I will not," Lionel insisted. "I have never thought you foolish. Not even when you climbed up that tree when we were fifteen to fetch conkers and broke your leg."

Lionel was gratified to see a smile flicker over his cousin's face as they turned a corner and made their way down a gravel path against the side of the house.

"I cannot wholly explain it," Adam confessed quietly, gazing at the grey sky above them.

"Are you unwell?" Lionel inquired, concern etched upon his features.

"No. No. Nothing like that, but I just experienced something... odd."

"I am intrigued."

"Lady Emilia Sterling was playing Bach's Fugue. The one mother always played."

"I know it well."

"It was her favourite. Usually, I would have walked *away* from the sound. The pianoforte brings such bad memories I tend to avoid it at all costs, but the way she played that piece. It filled my soul. As though my whole body had been dead for years and suddenly came alive. I have never heard anything like it, and I have heard that piece over one hundred times in my life."

Lionel remained quiet.

"I am overwrought," Adam continued. "I should not feel such things. The guilt is rising within me even as I think of it. To see a woman play my mother's song, just as Anastasia used to. I should not be entertaining such emotions. It is very wrong, and I do not know why it has overwhelmed me in such a way. I feel as though my mind is in twelve places at once."

"My dear fellow," Lionel began gently, "I would never presume to understand your grief, but it has been three years since Anastasia's death, and you have done little but work in the intervening time. Perhaps this is a sign that you are ready to rejoin the world, to allow yourself some relief. It could be as simple as enjoying music again, and that is a wonderful thing."

Adam glanced at him uncertainly, looking appearing all the more confused as they continued on their way.

"This party affords you a splendid opportunity to embrace some joy, Adam," Lionel insisted. "Anastasia would want you to live again. You cannot mourn her forever, and your mother would want you to enjoy something she loved without guilt." He clapped Adam on the shoulder. "None of this is a bad thing."

They had walked a loop of a small garden beside the house and both of them were making their way back to the main entrance without discussing it. Their breath was rising in great clouds all about them, and Lionel was already chilled to the bone.

"Perhaps you are right," Adam said with a rueful smile. "I confess, when we came here, I could not think of anything except getting through the next few days and returning to my office. Perhaps I *have* worked too hard and for too long and closed myself off from the simple pleasures life has to offer. But it was a foreign feeling, the exuberance her playing triggered in me."

"Of course. Of course it is, but do not fight it. The mind knows what it wants just as well as the heart, and perhaps it is telling you that you are ready for a new chapter. That is all."

Adam nodded as they entered the entrance hall, handing off their coats and red in the face from the frigid air.

"When did the blasted weather become so unaccommodating?" Lionel asked irritably, blowing into his hands and stamping his feet.

"I am going to get back to my warm chambers, and I shall see you at dinner," Adam said with a happier smile and Lionel watched him leave with what felt like hope in his chest.

A part of him was thrilled. Lady Emilia Sterling was a beautiful and talented woman. Lionel could not think of a better potential partner for his cousin but was under no illusions that he could expect anything from it.

For Adam, the world of love was a distant memory.

***

Emilia and Charlotte had repaired to Emilia's room to prepare for the ball.

Charlotte had brought a multitude of brooches and jewellery with her, which Emilia was admiring as she attempted to stop her hands from shaking.

Despite her worries and fears about socialising with so many strangers, Emilia could not deny that she was excited, too. The two of them had not attended a ball of such a large size together for many years, and the room was heavy with nervous energy.

To distract herself, Emilia had been telling Charlotte of the earl's strange behaviour that afternoon.

"What do you think he meant by it?" Charlotte mused.

Emilia loved her for many reasons, but the main one was that she was not a silly, giggling girl. Charlotte was reserved and measured in all things and never allowed herself to get carried away with idiotic fantasies.

"I do not know," Emilia replied. "He was watching me play, and then he turned away and almost ran from the room. What do *you* think it could mean?"

"I have heard you play many times, and you have quite enraptured me on several occasions. He may simply have admired your talents, of which there are many."

Charlotte pushed a beautiful pearl-encrusted comb into her hair and raised her eyebrows at Emilia for her opinion. Emilia nodded in approval, and Charlotte smiled demurely, happy that her friend seemed eager for the ball despite her concerns about how she would be received.

Emilia looked very lovely in a deep red gown that exactly matched the tiny bows she had placed in her hair. Charlotte watched her carefully in the mirror, considering what she had told her of the earl. She found herself intrigued.

It had been so many months since her friend had received even the slightest sniff of a prospect that they rarely spoke of men at all. Now, hearing of the earl's wide-eyed gaze and apparent interest, Charlotte was overjoyed for her friend. She did not wish to get carried away by the feeling, but it was encouraging nonetheless.

"Mama has asked me to perform this evening," Emilia added nervously.

"Well, that is wonderful, and so she should. You are by far the best pianist in the country," Charlotte said earnestly as Emilia rolled her eyes in the mirror.

"She has only asked me in order to impress Lord Elderbridge," Emilia said wearily, eyeing her friend nervously for any sign that Charlotte might have changed her mind about the match.

Charlotte glanced at her in the mirror's reflection and pursed her lips disapprovingly. "Mm. Do you think you could play everything in a minor key or dispense with every other note, perhaps? That might very well deter him."

"His daughters already hold me in deep disdain," Emilia said miserably.

"As much as I do not want you to marry the man, his daughters do not *know* you," Charlotte insisted. "Anyone who knows you loves you; it is to their detriment if they are uninterested in getting acquainted with you. I imagine in any other circumstances, you would get on very well together."

Both women stepped back to admire their finished ensembles in the mirror. Charlotte held out her hand to Emilia, and she took it as Charlotte fixed her with a stern glare.

"Remember the talent and strength you hold when you sit at the piano. That is all you should focus on. Tonight is an opportunity to perform again, nothing else. Do not think of the audience; think of your love of music. It has been a long time since you embraced playing again; let this be your chance to regain the joy you find in it." Charlotte smirked. "And do not focus on your audience. Focus on yourself. Although I will admit that your admirer is by far the most handsome man in the room, second only to his cousin."

Emilia watched Charlotte blush and laughed. "Lionel Spencer?" she asked teasingly, and Charlotte lifted her chin primly and waved her off as though it were nothing. "I had no idea you were interested in prospective suitors until the season begins."

"The marriage mart?" Charlotte exclaimed. "What rot! I merely said he was *handsome*. There are plenty of handsome men who are exceptionally stupid. He may not have any brains in his head; that is much more likely, and you know I cannot abide a bore."

Emilia snorted and shook her head as they headed downstairs together. It was the first ball of the Christmas period for her mother, and despite their strained relationship, Emilia was anxious that it went smoothly.

She tried to do as Charlotte had instructed, focusing on her performance and the fluttering of anticipation she felt ahead of it. But Emilia could not deny that a particular pair of piercing eyes were never far from her thoughts.

CHAPTER FIVE

The doors to the ballroom had been kept closed, even to the family, for two days.

Emilia had not known what her mother was planning, but she could scarcely believe her eyes when she entered the room.

If Christmas had not arrived in the rest of the house, it was certainly front and centre in the ballroom. Garlands hung from the mantelpiece, and holly had been placed all around the large mirror. The drinks table was filled with bowls of bright red punch, and holly leaves were sprinkled across it. Kissing boughs hung from the edge of the table, and ribbons in gold, green, and red danced throughout the room.

Emilia caught her mother's eye where she stood greeting her guests and saw a spark of her old self appear as she grinned in excitement. They had both always adored Christmas, and having the chance to show off the house with a ball was a wonderful thing.

The guests made their way inside, exclaiming at the beautiful décor; swathes of silk and velvet spun across Emilia's vision and everyone looked excited and jubilant chatter filling the air.

Emilia was surprised to find herself eagerly anticipating one man's entrance over all the others. The Earl of Bellebrook had intrigued her to such an extent that she could not get the man out of her mind. She wondered if he might address his odd behaviour, and a shiver of anticipation ran through her as she eagerly watched the doorway.

As her fingers plucked incessantly at the beading on her gown, her eyes fell on another newcomer to the ballroom. Lady Seraphina Cheswick glided into the room between her parents, the Marquess and Marchioness of Chesingdale. Everyone's attention was caught by their arrival; Seraphina looked like a swan in her white gown against the deep red and strict black of her mother and father.

Emilia's stomach tightened at the sight of them, but she quickly fixed a smile in place. She knew how important it was to her mother and father that the Chesingdale's had agreed to attend the ball, and it was imperative that she made a good impression. It seemed to Emilia that the whispers in the hall reached a crescendo, and she felt on display and ill at ease as she imagined everyone referencing her recent scandal.

She stood up straight, raised her chin, and refused to let slander and gossip influence her. She had never done anything wrong, and she intended to show the world that.

The ballroom was a lively prospect, and as they approached the doorway, Lionel's face lit up in a grin. Adam, on the other hand, felt nerves so strong that he thought he might cast up his accounts on the beautifully polished floor. To distract himself, Adam offered his arm to his aunt and manfully led her into the fray.

He was acutely aware that the one lady he had always relied upon was no longer on his arm. Anastasia had been a flawless companion at such functions, speaking when Adam had been tongue-tied and always ready to speak to anyone in her vicinity.

He had not realised how much he had relied upon her until he was suddenly amongst so many strangers. The room was brash, loud, and overcrowded. There were signs of Christmas everywhere, and the sight of them set his teeth on edge. Every tinkle of glass, raucous laugh, and the varied colours of rich greens and reds further cemented his wish to run quickly in the opposite direction and hide beneath a table in an empty room.

"Ah, there is Lady Seraphina. Does she not look well?"

Adam glanced at the lady. She was very beautiful in the way that many women of good breeding could be. She looked haughty in her expression, eyes narrowing at the dancefloor as though she were looking for anyone *worthy* enough to mark her card.

"I can see her, Aunt Augusta. Thank you for pointing her out," Adam replied as Lionel gave him a weary look over his mother's head.

Adam's gaze was drawn to their hosts. Lord and Lady Sternwood were speaking to the Pinkertons, an older couple who were well-known in society for their long and loving relationship and overly enthusiastic presence at almost every ball of the season. But as he watched Lord Pinkerton speaking with Lady Sternwood, another figure came into view.

Standing demure and quiet behind her mother, a dark red vision caught his eye.

Adam stared at Emilia as the fog of grief lifted, the notes from the pianoforte springing into his mind as though her face alone conjured the music. Her sharp features were framed beautifully by her hair, a lock of it tumbling past her high cheekbones. Those captivating eyes were looking toward the floor, her shoulders tense as she glanced about the room.

Adam looked away, discomfited and growing more irritable by the moment. She reminded him of Bach's melody. That lilting, rising ecstasy that became increasingly beautiful the more one listened to it.

This is quite ludicrous, he admonished himself; *I am no longer fifteen years old.*

"Must you appear so revolted by the place?" Augusta inquired sharply beside him. "It is *Christmas,* Adam. You are here to enjoy yourself. If you spend the entire fortnight with a face like thunder, no one will invite you to anything again."

Adam was not given the opportunity to respond to his aunt's harsh words, however, as suddenly there was a commotion at the doorway of the ballroom. They all turned to look at the man who had entered. Adam suppressed a curse at the sight of Mr Frederick Bentley, a connection long neglected and best forgotten.

Straight, tall, and formidable, Frederick Bentley was a distant paternal cousin of Adam's and was due to inherit the Bellebrook estate should Adam fail to produce an heir. Adam masked a grimace as he watched Frederick's charming smile illuminate the room. Adam knew all too well how deceiving it could be.

Frederick stood beside his mother, Mrs Verity Bentley, who was stooped and frail on his arm, peering about her with a look of confused interest. As they shook hands with the Sterlings, Adam heard Augusta tut beneath her breath.

"What in the world is Frederick doing here?" Augusta asked, sounding baffled.

"Mrs Verity is very close to Lady Camilla," Lionel muttered, keeping his voice low.

"Oh, of course, what rotten luck; they must have been invited to the house party as well. I declare I would never have come if I had known I would need to spend time with them in such close quarters."

There wasn't an ounce of truth in his aunt's words, of course. Adam knew she would have come regardless, but Frederick's presence would make the next few days even more trying for Adam, and he did not need any other reasons to want to run for the hills.

Frederick was handsome, and his manners afforded him many friends, but Adam knew of the darkness that resided within. The man was a veracious gambler and had squandered much of his own fortune at a young age in gambling hells about London.

His tongue and his face had afforded him some significant influence with certain members of the Ton, and he used their good feelings insatiably.

Adam knew he could ruin Frederick with a few words in the right ears if he so chose, but it was not in his nature to do so—even if he did intensely dislike the man.

Fredericks's eyes were already darting about the floor, seemingly assessing each woman as though he were looking at prizes at an auction. It wasn't long before Frederick spotted them and nodded. Adam knew they could not avoid speaking to the man.

"There is no avoiding it, I suppose," Augusta muttered, echoing Adam's thoughts perfectly.

"Frederick's propensity to shoot and play cards has won him many friends. Not to mention the fact that Lord Sternwood can afford to lose to him, they are regularly seen at White's playing piquet, so I'm told." Lionel's voice was a low murmur, but his eyes were sharp as he watched their cousin move toward them.

"Of course they are. Men will be men," Augusta grumbled, her mouth compressed in a firm line before she pasted a strained smile onto her face. "You will mark Lady Seraphina's card this evening, Adam," Augusta insisted, making the nerves roll through Adam's gut. "It is your duty to all of us never to allow that man anywhere near Bellebrook Manor. Is that understood?"

"Yes, Aunt," Adam replied resignedly, lamenting his position and wishing Anastasia were still there to defend him. Before he could be dragged back into the mire of his thoughts, however, Mr Frederick and his mother approached them. Frederick wore his patented supercilious smile, and his eyes didn't leave Adam's for a moment.

Mindful of his aunt's words, he affected a light smile. Even that tiny effort felt like it drained all of the energy from his body, and he could not wait to be alone in his bed chamber and hide under the covers until dawn.

"Lady Spencer, Lord Spencer, Lord Bellebrook," Frederick said as he bowed to them all. "I had no idea you were attending this event, and I am so pleased to be able to spend some quality time with such esteemed members of my family."

His mother's eyes were adoring as she looked at her son. Everything Frederick did was perfect in the eyes of Mrs Bentley and Adam knew she was unaware of his gambling debts.

Frederick's short black hair had been slicked back, showing off his prominent features. He had very pale blue eyes, a wide smile, straight white teeth and a perpetually amused expression.

When Adam was younger, Frederick's charm and charisma had quickly deceived him, as it did to many. They had been firm friends in their early teens, but it had not taken long for Adam to understand his true nature. Frederick acted for himself alone and had little regard for anything but the expansion of his fortunes. His gaze was calculating, and behind it was a hint of challenge, but Adam kept his smile in place.

"Frederick, it's a pleasure to have you with us once more," Adam said, his tone courteous but lacking true warmth. He turned to Mrs Verity Bentley with a polite, restrained smile. "And Mrs Bentley, how are you faring? I had heard you were quite unwell in the autumn."

Mrs Bentley's rather vacant expression turned to him, and she smiled wanly. "Indeed, I was most unwell, but my son cared for me every day. He is the very best of men."

Adam felt his aunt stiffen considerably and nodded to Frederick. "A noble thing to do, I am sure. Will you be staying for the events to come?"

"Most certainly. Lady Sternwood has been adamant that I should remain for everything," he leaned in close, affecting a humble expression. "I do not believe Lord Sternwood would hold this gathering without me." He leaned back again, smug in his own self-importance, and Adam struggled to stop himself from rolling his eyes.

"We are delighted you are here," Augusta said, sounding so sincere that Adam was rather taken aback.

His gaze wandered as Mrs Bentley and his aunt began speaking of the beauty of the room, falling once again on the demure and stunning woman on the edge of it. It occurred to Adam in that moment that Lady Emilia Sterling was by far the most beautiful creature he had ever laid eyes on.

***

Emilia's fingers fluttered at her skirts as she waited for the guests to settle before taking her seat at the pianoforte.

Her mother had arranged a small performance before the ball began. She could hear the odd chord from a cello and the trill of a violin from the other room as the players began setting up for the dance ahead.

She noticed the tall form of Lord Bellebrook at the back of the room as he leaned down to speak with his aunt. He was accompanied by the man Charlotte had spoken of earlier in the day, and Emilia could quite see how she might like the look of him. His dark hair was a contrast to Bellebrook's ash-blond style, but their eyes were almost identical in colour. Emilia realised she was staring and swiftly looked away.

Her fingers trembled slightly as she looked at the keys, all of the nightmares and shadows of her past threatening to weigh her down. Everyone in the room was impossibly still, as though they were all holding their breath. A cruel part of her mind conjured images of women gripping the hands of their husbands, knowing of her reputation and attempting to protect their men from her influence.

She closed her eyes, trying to settle her thundering heartbeat. The piece she had chosen was one of Beethoven's more difficult melodies. She knew she would need a challenge to occupy her in the weeks leading up to the event, and she had practised for hours to ensure that she could play it perfectly.

She took a deep breath, memorising the beginning few bars of the sheet music ahead of her, and placing her fingers gently on the cold keys.

As she began to play, she was gratified when the old feelings flooded back. The world faded away, and all that existed was her fingers on the piano and the music rising and falling, her whole body singing with it as though a part of her came alive at its presence.

Her fears, her hopes and her longing for acceptance danced through the bars and over the notes as she continued to play. The piece spoke of the joy of the Christmas season, the excitement that she had once felt at this sacred time, and her own desperate urge to be seen.

As she played, Emilia fantasised that the music itself might somehow wash away the stain of scandal, and she would be reborn anew.

CHAPTER SIX

Adam stood at the back of the room and tried to keep the tears from falling down his cheeks. It now seemed foolish to have deprived himself of such rapture for all these years.

The music filled his soul, his mind and body transfixed by the woman before him. Emilia's talents for the pianoforte were unsurpassed, at least in the company that Adam kept. Even some of the professional concerts he had been to paled by comparison.

It was not just her precise and fluid technique that made the music seem to become a part of her, but the expressions and passion that danced across her face. She moved with the music, her eyes closed, barely needing to refer to the sheet in front of her at all. She became one with the instrument as though she were carved as part of the piano itself.

Despite his best efforts, Adam felt a tear break free, tracing a path down his cheek. It was as though, in the pit of his stomach, a cauldron of emotions had lurked for months with the lid tightly fastened. Now, as the music sent a tendril of joy and happiness through the room, the spiralling fingers of it prized open the lid, and everything began to burst free.

The music spoke of loss, resilience, light, and beauty that persists, even in the darkest depths of despair. For the first time since Anastasia's death, Adam felt a spark of something bright and new ignite within him. It was a trembling, terrifying moment of recognition, surrounded by a room full of strangers, most of whom were listening with interest and admiration, but *nothing* of the soaring ecstasy Adam felt.

Time seemed to slow, the air thickening and growing stiflingly warm as the figure before him transformed. It was no longer Emilia at the pianoforte but Anastasia—clear as day, impossibly vivid, and achingly beautiful. Her fingers glided over the keys, her voice humming softly in tune, and her form swayed in tender harmony with the melody.

Then she raised her gaze, and Adam's heart stilled in that breathless, timeless moment that seemed to stretch into eternity.

How he had longed to see that kind gaze again, to look upon her gentle face and witness the warmth in her eyes once more. She leaned back, her fingers still playing, and she laughed. It was a high, magnificent sound that seemed to transcend the space, and for the first time, her memory did not trigger pain. Adam could feel the sadness, as he had always done—perhaps he always would—but beneath it, there was something else now. Under the chaos of his sorrow and grief was an undercurrent of bright, tender joy, and he allowed it to touch his heart as the tears fell in earnest.

Then the music stopped, and reality snapped back into place.

Emilia lifted her fingers from the keys and breathed a sigh of relief. The room erupted with applause from every quarter, and she rose, making a small courtesy to the company. She felt elated by her performance—not quite renewed, but certainly, as though she had proved her talents once more.

Her relief and gratitude were extinguished, however, when the Duke of Elderbridge immediately approached in front of her audience, eclipsing them from view with a smile that looked more like a smirk.

It is almost as though he is pleased with me. She thought. *As though he were a tutor, and I had passed the first test.*

He bowed to her, and she curtsied quickly, aware of how many eyes were now upon them.

"Lady Emilia, that was superb. " His deep voice grated at the back of his throat.

She forced a smile. "Thank you, your Grace. There is nothing I enjoy more than playing."

"And performing. You are very talented indeed."

She felt the heat of an infuriating blush suffuse her cheeks. To anyone watching them, it would look like she was blushing at a compliment. In truth, she was merely out of practice at taking them. She wanted to stamp her foot in frustration as a knowing gleam entered his eyes.

Can this man truly believe I am interested in him? He is old enough to be my father.

"I would request the first dance from you, my Lady. I have never been so pleased to be in the company of such a partner."

The thought of allowing him to dance with her made her skin crawl, but she would not embarrass her mother and father in such a public setting.

"Of course, your Grace, I would be delighted," she managed as her eyes flitted across the room to look at her parents. Her mother had her hands clasped before her in apparent glee, and her father looked exceedingly proud.

They are not proud of me for my playing. They are proud that my music has finally attracted a suitor.

There was a bitter taste in her mouth as the Duke of Elderbridge took her arm, and the crowd parted for them as though they were newlyweds.

They walked back toward the ballroom, the duke saying nothing on the journey as the bustle and babble of the crowd followed them over the highly polished floors of the entrance hall.

Entering the room, Emilia noticed the group of players in the corner were awaiting their arrival and as soon as she set foot inside, they began to play a waltz. Emilia glanced back at her mother, enraged at the possibility that this had all been by design, but her look of fury was wasted as her mother was whispering rapidly in her father's ear.

She turned back to the floor and tried her best to relax. The worst thing she could do was put the duke off entirely. If she were too obvious with her innermost feelings, every single guest would observe it in an instant. Despite her own disgust at the match, anyone else in high society would see the duke as an ideal husband for her. She had to tread carefully to ensure she did not disgrace herself further.

As the rest of the couples congregated, Emilia felt the duke's fingers settle in the small of her back and take her hand in his. She deliberately lowered her shoulders, trying to keep her face neutral as they began to move.

Passing around the edge of the dancefloor, Emilia felt a prickling at the back of her neck as though someone were watching her. Her face felt hot and uncomfortable, and she discreetly tried to glance at the crowd.

At the edge of the room, all three of the duke's daughters were standing in a line, like Grecian statues, staring at their father as he passed them. Emilia averted her gaze instantly, but the eldest, Sophia, had narrowed eyes, her fingers gripping the fan in her hands so tightly that she might break it. Penelope and Caroline whispered together incessantly, their eyes travelling over Emilia's figure and making her miss a step in the dance.

The duke's fingers tightened immediately around her, and Emilia endeavoured to regain her composure. To refuse the dance would have been unthinkable, yet now the implications of it seemed far worse. She was flooded with anxiety as she considered how this might look. With two weeks of the house party ahead of them, the duke would have no obstacles in his pursuit of her. She could not imagine how she would repel every single advance without causing offence.

"You are an excellent dancer," the duke said, that same strange smile on his lips. Emilia didn't believe he was intending to smirk, but he had a look of laughing arrogance that didn't come over well.

"Thank you, your Grace, as are you," she replied, trying to pull her fingers from his grip. His hand was tightening at every pass they made.

"I am pleased to be able to make your acquaintance finally," he murmured, the smell of brandy wafting over Emilia's face unpleasantly. "I have long admired your father and felt that a match within his household would be most fitting." Emilia smiled faintly, fixing her gaze just to the right of his ear. "As you know, your father is cursed with the same predicament as I."

"Your Grace?"

"Too many daughters," he said, as though it were a great joke. "Lord Sternwood knows the pain of never birthing a son. I believe you would make an excellent mother to my girls, and my hope is that my curse will soon be lifted."

Emilia stared at him, astounded by his audacity. Though she was her father's only child, the duke's words implied that even she was of little worth compared to a son. And so here he was, during the very first dance of the season—their first true conversation—already speaking of his need for an heir. The room felt suddenly smaller, the distant chatter growing faint as her pulse quickened. His eyes held a smug certainty as though the marriage had already been agreed upon. She swallowed hard, bile rising in her throat. The prospect of a future with him felt suffocating, the very idea causing her skin to prickle with unease.

As Emilia attempted to keep her poise and twirled about the floor with the duke, Adam was having his own troubles.

Leaving the drawing room had been more complicated than it should have been. The tears on his cheeks were certainly not mirrored by anyone else. No other man or woman had been so affected by the piece, and Adam was forced to discreetly wipe at his eyes before leaving the room.

Turning, he found Lionel standing behind him, shielding him from view. His cousin had evidently seen his emotional state and taken it upon himself to protect him from prying questions. Adam gave Lionel a grateful nod, and his cousin returned it with a concerned expression.

As soon as Lionel had departed, however, Adam was approached by Lady Seraphina Cheswick. She was searching for her handkerchief, which she said she had accidentally dropped; however, Adam was unsurprised to find it with ease, just beside his shoe. As he returned it to her, there was a charged moment of expectation—her parents stood nearby, watching them intently.

They approached Adam and their daughter, the Marchioness inclining her head with a gracious smile. "Allow us to introduce ourselves; I am Lady Chesingdale, and this is my husband, the Marquess. It is our distinct pleasure to present our daughter, Lady Seraphina." After exchanging the usual courtesies, it seemed only fitting that he should ask her for a dance.

However, now that they turned on their third go-around on the floor, Adam would happily have switched partners with anyone else in the room.

"Oh, I have much to be grateful for, my Lord," Lady Seraphina was saying. "I have such a wonderful abundance of friends in Bath, you know. Have you ever been to Bath, my Lord?"

"Yes, when I was—"

"It is the most wonderful city on Earth. I do believe that if I should ever marry, I would wish to live there. Have you taken the waters? They were so restorative. I was so intrigued by the Roman baths and how the people had once lived. I was being told the most amazing story by a friend of mine, do you know Lady Viola Templeton?"

"I do not belie—"

"She is the daughter of the Duke of Hastings, lately married. Such a wonderful patron of the arts. She was the first to introduce me to the Roman Baths and is the greatest authority on such things."

And so it continued for the whole of the dance.

Adam had tried to participate in the conversation at first but soon gave up, allowing the young lady to prattle on. He didn't want to judge her too harshly—Lady Seraphina seemed just as nervous as he was—but she spoke so incessantly that he could barely get a word in.

Her conversation revolved entirely around the latest gossip, making her appear frivolous and lacking in intelligence. Worse still, she seemed utterly unaware of how tiresome she was.

His attention had drifted several times to the other couples on the floor and found himself searching out Lady Emilia in the throng.

She had beautiful form and almost faultless steps, but her smile was insincere, her back stiff and rigid against the duke. Adam thought Lady Emilia may not be too fond of her dance partner. She was leaning subtly away from him, and whereas Emilia's feet were sure and perfect, the duke was a little clumsier in his bearing. His nose was rather pink, as were his cheeks, a sure sign of too much brandy before dinner.

Adam felt a surge of protectiveness at the sight of her discomfort. Watching her delicate fingers flex against the duke's wide, bulbous shoulders seemed wrong somehow. He tried to focus on what Lady Seraphina was saying to him, but it was no use. The more he watched Emilia, the more her discomfort became apparent.

"Do you not think so, my Lord?" Adam looked back at Seraphina's upturned, expectant face and felt a bolt of panic. *What had she been saying?*

"Yes, quite," he attempted, and her eyes lit up at his answer. He wasn't sure what he had agreed to.

"Are you remaining at the house for the party to follow?"

"Indeed, are you?"

"I am," she ran her eyes over his hair and back to his face. "I am most pleased that I will be able to get to know you better, my Lord," she added with a coquettish smile.

"Likewise," he added automatically as they passed his aunt, watching them happily from the edge of the room.

Adam inwardly shook himself, trying to dispel the overwhelming feeling of protectiveness he felt for Lady Emilia. It was not simply that he wished to shield her from the duke; there was also a faint glimmer of something else at the back of his mind that felt alarmingly like jealousy.

He was unsure why he felt such a need to be near her or why his heart picked up whenever she entered a room. Adam was certain it was merely misplaced affection for his fond memories of the music she played. It would pass; he was sure of it.

It has to.

As the dance neared its end there was one more couple on the floor, who knew nothing of the discomfort Emilia and Adam were feeling.

In his eagerness to dance, an activity he greatly loved, Lionel had decided to mark the cards of as many eligible ladies as he could.

Having observed Adam's sadness at the performance, Lionel had intended to pull his cousin aside and ensure he was well, but his infernal mother had somehow achieved her aim, and Adam was now standing up with Lady Seraphina.

In turn, Lionel thought he might invite Emilia for a dance, but the duke had beaten him to it. Turning to see if his mother was still interfering his eyes had alighted on a sparkling comb hanging loosely from the hair of Emilia's friend. He had wracked his brain to remember her name and miraculously recalled she was a *Miss Fairfax.*

To his shame, he had not paid much attention to anyone but Lady Emilia in the first moments of the ball. She was an exquisite musician, and Lionel hadn't remembered a performance he had enjoyed so much in recent memory. He had scarcely acknowledged Miss Fairfax, and now, he was quite irritated with himself for not having given her more attention.

Miss Fairfax was uncommonly pretty, with eyes that reminded Lionel of honey—his favourite food.

He approached her, feeling rather awkward, and cleared his throat. As she turned, the comb, which was already loose, flew out of her hair, and he was rather proud of himself for catching it effortlessly and giving her a winning smile.

"Miss Fairfax, I believe it is frowned upon to hurl combs at guests without any warning."

To his ultimate joy, she neither blushed nor apologised but raised an eyebrow in challenge.

"Well, my Lord, it is frowned upon to *appropriate* a lady's possessions, so I suppose we are at an impasse."

Lionel found himself laughing heartily at that. He quickly offered to replace the comb, muttering continually about his lack of expertise, and the final result was rather crooked. One swift movement from the lady, however, and it was perfectly straight again. She had long, very dark hair, which shimmered in the candlelight, and her eyes were flecked with copper as he looked at them.

"In light of my behaviour and stealing from you when we are not yet fully acquainted, may I ask to make amends by requesting you join me in a dance?"

Her expressive eyes twinkled at him. "I should be delighted."

"It is Miss Charlotte Fairfax I am addressing?" he confirmed, always a little uncertain he could remember a name correctly.

"Yes, Lord Spencer. We met once a few years ago I recall. I hear you are very fond of dancing."

"My reputation precedes me, I see. With the right partner, a dance can be most diverting."

"I shall have to ensure that I come up to muster then," she replied mischievously, and Lionel grinned down at her as they made their way onto the floor.

He found they had a great deal in common, and he had not enjoyed himself so much in weeks. Though reserved in manners and impeccably polite, when not under the heavy gaze of her mother, Charlotte came to life.

They discussed literature, of which they had a shared love, and Lionel learned that she had a cat named Fergus, who she adored. His mother also had a cat named Mischief, who was constantly causing havoc, and they had a merry time enthusing over their feline companions throughout the rest of the dance.

The next set was a quadrille and necessitated the need for new partners. Adam had never felt such relief to be released from Lady Seraphina's company; the lady had scarcely paused for breath in five minutes together.

His relief was quickly obliterated by nerves, however, as Emilia Sterling became his partner. As she stepped into his arms and they took up the well-ingrained positions of the dance, Adam found it difficult to breathe.

How odd she must think me, for my behaviour when we first arrived.

He tried not to stare, but now that he was closer to her, she was even more exquisite than he had thought. Her lips kicked up into a gentle smile, her skin soft and glowing, and he was gratified to find that her body was entirely relaxed against him—nothing like it had been with the duke.

"You must think me terribly odd," he said eventually when he could stand the silence no longer.

"My Lord?" she asked, looking confused.

"I am aware that you saw me watching you play this afternoon. I apologise if I came across as rude with my abrupt departure; I was enchanted by the music. I love that piece and had not heard it for some time."

A faint flush suffused her cheeks, and Adam watched it with fascination.

"I did not think you odd," she said with a slight frown. "I wondered if perhaps my playing had caused you to leave; I was only practising, after all."

That startled a laugh out of Adam, and a few people nearby turned to stare at him. "I do not believe for a moment that anyone could find your playing *offensive*. You have a true gift for the pianoforte. I have never heard a performance like it."

"You enjoyed it then?"

The hesitancy in her words gave him pause, and he looked down at her in surprise. Their gazes caught, and all the reassurance he wished to provide her with seemed to pour through that look and mix between them.

"Very much," he said softly. "I have not allowed myself to listen to music often in recent months. It has some painful memories, but I believe I could listen to you play that piece, or any piece, all day long without losing interest."

Emilia's heart fluttered in her chest as she listened to Adam's words. She had always been told she had a talent for music, but there was something in how he expressed it that made her truly believe it.

"Do you play?" she asked.

"No, I confess, I have never had much talent for music. I believe my mother wished to burn my violin when I was a lad."

She laughed lightly as they briefly swapped partners with the other couple in their group, and he watched her elegantly navigate the steps.

"You are a talented performer."

"Thank you, my Lord. I have often wished to compose my own music, but I cannot help but compare it with the masters. My own tinkling tunes seem too simplistic by comparison."

Adam moved through the centre of the square and out again, the two couples coming together once more.

"I can understand your hesitancy, but one can never achieve anything for fear of failure."

"You are right, of course. Perhaps once the season is over, I shall try to revive my old pieces."

"I should like to hear them," Adam said eagerly, realising he meant it. Unlike his automatic responses to Seraphina Cheswick, there was no pretence with Lady Emilia. Her bright eyes sparked as she looked up at him, and Adam's heart was pounding so loudly that he wondered if it did not drown out the lively music all around them.

From the other side of the dancefloor, unobserved and partnerless for a short while, Frederick Bentley watched Adam moving across the floor with Emilia and tried not to snap the stem of his glass.

Adam's movements had changed considerably since he'd been dancing with the Cheswick chit. He was more fluid now, happier, lighter on his feet, and that was a worrying sign. Frederick's teeth dug into his lip as his eyes followed them around the room. Emilia, in turn, was all smiling openness around Adam, and Frederick's shoulders tightened incrementally at each pass about the floor.

"I have such hopes for him."

Frederick's ears pricked up as he noticed Lady Spencer, Augusta standing beside Lady Sternwood, watching the dancing couple just as he had done.

"I long to see Adam happily married again after the losses in his life. He deserves to find contentment once more."

"I couldn't agree more," Lady Sternwood replied, "such an affable and kind man; I would wish him nothing but happiness and am so glad he could attend our little party."

Frederick took a sip of his wine. The prospect of Adam marrying again was a terrible blow that he had not anticipated.

Why can't the man remain locked in his study for the rest of time and wither away as I had expected?

Adam had not been seen outside the house for years, and suddenly, Frederick had walked into the ballroom to find him looking better than ever. The last he had heard, Adam was two steps from a nervous collapse, and Frederick had been waiting in the wings ever since.

Now, he looked like a spritely youth, a faint smile on his lips, poised and collected. It was infuriating. If Adam were allowed to remain in Lady Emilia's company for too long, Frederick could well imagine an attachment forming between them—and with it, his hopes of inheriting the earldom would be dashed forever. He could not afford to let such a prospect unfold.

His throat tightened around a nervous swallow as he thought of the debts awaiting repayment back in London, and his resolve sharpened.

Moving slowly through the crowd, nodding to each vague acquaintance and keeping a bland smile on his face, he considered his options carefully.

Positioning himself behind the Duke of Elderbridge and his prim, priggish daughters, Frederick observed the duke watching Lady Emilia. The man had the expression of someone who had already staked his claim on her.

A plan slowly formed in the back of Frederick's mind, and he sipped his drink, realising that there may well be a way to ensure that they could be pulled apart forever.

That is the trouble with scandal, Frederick thought happily; *it never fully fades away.*

CHAPTER SEVEN

After the joy of the dance with Lord Bellebrook, Emilia was elated. As he led her from the floor, returning her to her mother and father with a perfect bow, Emilia tried to conceal the blush she knew was painted across her face.

Her mother watched their approach excitedly and smiled as Lord Bellebrook removed himself from their company.

"I am most pleased, Emilia, " her mother exclaimed as she watched Adam's back glide through the crowd. "He is such an excellent dance partner."

"Do you think so, Mama?"

"Of course! And his daughters are the most elegant women, are they not? Why, I believe the duke is already taken with you. You must ensure that you use the Christmas party to get to know him."

Emilia clenched her fists at her sides. Her association with Lord Bellebrook might be fleeting, but he was at least someone she could look forward to spending time within the coming days. The duke was the opposite of that. Smelling of brandy and constantly followed about by his judgmental daughters, Emilia had no desire to spend more time with him than was necessary.

To her dismay, the decision was taken out of her hands while she was at the refreshment table. She had been admiring the kissing boughs and the effort her mother had put into them when a light touch to her elbow made her turn, and her stomach plummeted to the floor.

It was evident the Duke of Elderbridge had indulged in more alcohol since the dance. His eyes were glassy, and his jaw wobbled beneath his beard as he smiled at her. Emilia had an uncle who drank heavily, and she recognised the signs of a man who pretended to be sober in public, even when he was not.

"Your Grace," she greeted him with a tight smile.

"You are in need of refreshment, I see," he said as though it were an impressive observation. "One mustn't drink too much at these sorts of things, of course, no matter your nerves."

The absolute hypocrisy of the man, she thought furiously.

"Indeed, my Lord, I am drinking the fruit cordial only."

"Good girl," he said, reaching for the decanter of wine. It was tied beautifully with a red ribbon trimmed with gold. As the duke's meaty fingers seized upon it, the bow fell forlornly to the surface of the table, where it absorbed the splash of wine he then managed to spill across it.

I could never desire this man, she thought desperately. *How can my parents believe he is a suitable husband for me?*

She wanted to tell him to leave her alone, to turn her back and cut him completely, but her options were limited. She could not simply brush him off. If he chose to make an offer to her father, she knew it would be accepted without question. Given her current status in society, turning down a duke's proposal was almost impossible.

She felt increasingly ensnared by the events spiralling around her, a mounting sense of fear taking hold. Her life no longer felt her own, as though she were merely a spectator to her own fate.

Across the room, Adam watched Emilia flinch away from the duke and felt an overwhelming urge to intervene. She looked miserable.

He had wondered whether Lady Emilia approved of the duke's attentions, given their age difference. Elderbridge was wealthy, to be sure, but there were over twenty years between them. Adam knew plenty of mothers who would prefer a younger candidate to secure a good marriage.

He had been surprised, therefore, to see Lady Sternwood's enthusiasm for the match. She had barely spared Adam a glance when he had returned from the dancefloor.

He frowned as the duke swayed alarmingly toward Lady Emilia, his body brushing against hers. Her back stiffened visibly, her eyes glazing over as though she were picturing herself somewhere else. Adam was desperate to step in so she might escape.

He took a step forward, determined to follow through with his plan. However, just as he did so, Anastasia's face loomed in his memory, and he felt a jolt of intense guilt. He stopped, paralyzed by grief and indecision.

This is not my place. Her affairs are not my concern, and I must not presume she would welcome my interference in any case.

Having convinced himself his services were unnecessary, he turned away, burying his discomfort in a glass of wine.

***

As the ball transitioned to a formal dinner, Adam found himself seated beside Lady Seraphina Cheswick. It certainly felt deliberate this time, and he glanced up the table at his aunt, irritated that she continued to manipulate him, even when they were not at home.

Lady Seraphina was the height of gentility and polite, aristocratic conversation. Before Adam could sit down, she had commented upon the cutlery, the pinecones placed beside the fire in the scuttle, and almost every napkin on the table.

The conversation remained stilted and awkward as Adam struggled for an interesting topic, acutely aware of all the other guests conversing easily around them.

"Have you travelled much, my Lord?" Seraphina asked as the starters were served.

"Not in recent years, but I did travel extensively in my youth."

"I adore travelling, although I am not so comfortable on a ship. My stomach does not agree with the jostling of the sea," she tittered in a way that might have been pretty if it weren't at such a high pitch.

Adam glanced down the table to where Emilia was seated. She was opposite her friend Miss Fairfax and sitting beside Lionel. The three of them were in a lively debate, and Adam was rather envious of their easy conversation.

He allowed Lady Seraphina's constant stream of chatter to fade into the background and, as discreetly as possible, began to eavesdrop upon the group's discussion.

"Miss Fairfax has always been a terrible influence," Emilia was saying over the protestations of her friend. "She once took me down to the side of a lake near her home and pushed me in."

"I did no such thing. This is slander!" Miss Fairfax exclaimed.

Emilia was smiling heartily now. "There is a sordid rumour that I fell, but I maintain I was pushed. She also led me into a cave once!"

Adam found himself smiling. Emilia seemed to be telling the tales for Lionel's benefit, who had barely taken his eyes from Miss Fairfax.

"A cave?" Lionel asked, taking a sip of his wine as Charlotte tried to contain her laughter.

"It was not a *cave;* it was a small overhang beneath the rocks, and I thought I had seen a den beneath it."

"Wolves, no doubt," Emilia said darkly.

"Wolves do not dwell in caverns, nor do they roam England!" Miss Fairfax protested and all of them fell about laughing. Adam could not help but smile along with them.

"My Lord?"

Adam looked back to his dinner partner. Seraphina's eyes flickered between his and Lady Emilia's, her smile seeming rather more fixed than it had been.

"Yes, my Lady?"

"I was asking you where you had travelled to," she seemed crestfallen. "That is what we were discussing."

"Of course. Yes. I believe my favourite destination is Paris. What is yours?"

Seraphina Cheswick seemed to recover herself a little and began speaking of Bath again, whilst Adam tried to look interested in the topic. Without conscious thought his mind began to imagine showing Lady Emilia Paris. He had always intended to go with Anastasia, but her illness had prevented it. He wondered what Lady Emilia would think of the beauty he found there, his love of the city and its artwork, not to mention its music.

"I have always longed to go to Paris," Seraphina concluded, drinking the last of her wine, her cheeks slightly flushed.

"I am sure you would adore the city. And there is nothing to prevent more travelling in later life," he mused. Perhaps he might return to Paris someday; he had missed it.

The look on Seraphina's face transformed instantly into happy joy, and Adam's gut clenched as he saw her mother looking at them meaningfully. The marchioness was watching them with a gleam in her eyes, and Adam placed his glass on the table, grinding his teeth.

This was precisely why he had wanted to avoid such a party. Every interaction became something to remark upon between a man and a woman at this kind of occasion. He could not even have an innocent discussion on travel without others assuming he was pursuing a new match.

He looked around the table, observing the machinations of the society he had been separated from for so long. Every interaction, when observed from a distance, had a double meaning. Ladies who were polite to one another were often rivals, vying to get their daughter married to the same man.

All of the men were pontificating about their accomplishments—Frederick and the duke included. It reminded Adam of a nest of vipers trying to eat each other to become the strongest versions of themselves.

As Lady Seraphina began speaking of the many candles on the table and how exquisite the decorations were, Adam allowed his gaze to wander, taking in Lady Emilia's laugh and her bright, twinkling eyes.

As she took a sip from her glass, Emilia was aware of the earl observing her and felt a fluttering in her chest at his scrutiny. She had been rather downcast to see him sitting with Lady Seraphina at the table but Lord Spencer was excellent company.

She was pleased that he seemed to have eyes only for Charlotte. They were a handsome couple, with Charlotte's dark hair matching that of Lord Spencer. Both of them were tall and elegant and he was clearly intelligent which would please her friend.

As Lord Spencer and Charlotte spoke together, they touched upon a topic that Emilia was less familiar with. Both of them adored the book Gulliver's Travels, which Emilia had yet to read. As she allowed them to have their time in relative privacy, her ears were attuned to another conversation further down the table, where Caroline, Penelope, and Sophia Easton were sitting with their father.

Emilia had been relieved not to be placed beside the duke at dinner, but now she realised her foolishness in assuming she would escape his attentions entirely.

"But this is the issue, is it not?" Sophia asked loudly, her fork hovering above her plate with a perfect cube of meat speared on the end of it. "Scandal dogs one's steps forever. There is no escaping it. A good name can be tarnished for all time by the slightest misstep."

"Indeed," Penelope agreed, sounding older than her years. "I knew of a girl who merely *looked* at an eligible man the wrong way before she was out in society, and no one would go near her again!"

Emilia kept her back straight, and her head bowed over her food. She did not look in their direction, forcing the embarrassment of the topic away.

"Scandal can be forgiven if it is far enough in the past," the duke interjected. He had barely spoken until that moment, and his interruption felt pointed. Emilia would have given anything to leave the room.

"Yes, Papa, but who would wish to be tainted by it? When Joselyn Mortimer was disgraced, I had to cut her from my circle. And she was my *dearest* friend," Sophia stated.

Emilia recognised that tone. It was the sort of thing people said when the subject of their conversation was not *dear* at all.

"It depends upon the nature of the scandal," the duke concluded dismissively. "Many are overblown."

Emilia wasn't sure if he thought he was helping her with that comment, but she hated it all the same. It could not be a coincidence that the topic had been raised within her earshot. She did not wish to actively think ill of people, but his daughters appeared to be making a deliberate point for her benefit.

Two years before, the duke's defence of her might have been a touching thing to hear. But now, his comments on her apparent loss of virtue made her hackles rise.

I do not need defending because I have done nothing wrong. If the vultures in society had not listened to Henrietta, I would not have had to endure this idiocy.

She wished she could say something, even stand and address them haughtily, and then stalk out of the room. But she knew it would be pointless—the only person she would end up injuring would be herself.

Across the table, Charlotte observed her friend trying to keep her own temper in check. The duke's daughters really did seem to be the worst type of women. So far, Charlotte had seen nothing but cynical looks, unpleasant commentary, and superiority from the lot of them.

Charlotte had always admired Emilia for her resilience in weathering the cruel storm that had swirled about her for so long. As their gazes met, she raised her eyebrows in a silent query to ensure that Emilia was alright, but her friend merely shook her head in reply.

Charlotte's eyes were drawn to the man to Emilia's right, his gaze occasionally flicking over to the duke's daughters with what looked like veiled annoyance.

Charlotte had been quite mistaken in her dismissal of him. Lionel Spencer was anything but a simpleton. He was intelligent, witty, very handsome and altogether the type of man she enjoyed spending time with.

However, Charlotte felt a shudder of something foreign and alarming as she looked at him.

Her mother and father had told her many times that her conduct was the reason she had never attracted a man in her first season. Indeed, she had had no prospects for the majority of the summer and no callers. Charlotte's fingers clenched around her knife and fork as she recalled the endless days, sitting beside her mother upon the settee, waiting for visitors who never came.

She stared down at her plate, scolding herself for her wayward thoughts.

What would a man like Lionel Spencer see in the likes of me?

***

As the dinner concluded and the party dispersed, many of the ladies appeared relieved to part from the gentlemen for a while. The men made their way to the billiards room, while the ladies withdrew to the drawing room.

Unfortunately, Emilia found herself seated beside Sophie and Penelope again, and her mother was nowhere to be found. Emilia was suddenly isolated and alone amidst a group of strangers, and Penelope took full advantage, turning to her sister pointedly as she glanced at Emilia.

"I saw the Countess of Blackmoor at the Yule Ball a few days ago."

Emilia's spine went rigid.

"Oh, she is the kindest creature in the world," Sophia replied. "I adore the balls that she arranges; they are the best events of the season." Sophia turned to Emilia. "Did you attend the ball, Lady Emilia?"

Emilia felt as though she were looking down the barrel of a musket, and every single eye in the room had turned to stare at her.

The absolute audacity of Penelope. She was likely not even old enough to know of the scandal; she would only have heard of it from her sister.

"Sadly, not," Emilia managed, "we were unable to attend as my father was out of the country."

"What a pity. I understood you were acquainted with the countess."

Sophia was playing a dangerous game; even Emilia knew that. The embarrassment was all her own, but openly discussing a scandal in such a way was generally frowned upon. The *Ton* were much more comfortable speaking behind a person's back than challenging them outright. But

Sophia was clever enough to keep her tone innocent and light. It was clever; even Emilia had to admit that.

"I am acquainted with her," Emilia said. She was tempted to add, 'and her son, Lord Julian,' to see if Sophia recoiled behind her barb, but she knew that would be beyond foolish.

"Yes, I am sure she has mentioned your name to me," Sophia added, her eyes narrowing as though trying to remember. "And, of course, she is a great friend of Papa's, and he values her opinion above all others."

Emilia nodded, unable to speak. Was this girl honestly referring to her connection with the duke before they had even spent a full day together? She must have nerves of steel.

Or perhaps she simply does not care.

Emilia glanced around at the other women in the circle and was dismayed to find that no one would meet her eyes. The scandal she had hoped would be so far in her past that many would overlook it was hanging between them all like a shroud.

She forced a tight smile.

"It is rather close in here; I shall just get some air by the window," she muttered and rose, forcing herself to walk slowly away from the group instead of breaking into a run.

As she came to the window ledge, she stared out at the muted white blanket that lay across the grass in the gardens. Snow had been steadily falling throughout the ball, and it was beyond beautiful to watch it in the reflections of the firelight. Emilia wished she were outside, experiencing the first fall of winter alone. She loved being by herself. There was no one to judge her or pity her. She could just be.

"I did not know it was snowing," Charlotte remarked as she made her way over to her friend. She had just entered the room and was surprised to find Emilia alone. "It is so beautiful."

"Mm," Emilia said softly.

"I cannot believe how agreeable Lord Spencer is. I feel rather foolish, having assumed he would be a dullard. Do you know he has read almost as many books as I have? Including the love stories that I thought most men would not be interested in at all. His favourite book is Emma by Jane Austen, just like mine. I do not remember when anyone has made me smile so much." She laughed. "You are wicked for saying I pushed you into that lake. If I *had* pushed you in I would not have been so wet trying to get you *out*."

Charlotte paused when she noticed that her friend did not appear to be listening to her. Her eyes were glazed, and her skin was rather pale.

"Emilia?" she asked. "Are you alright?"

"Yes, yes," Emilia said blithely, pushing away the melancholy of her situation. She looked at Charlotte's wide hazel eyes and the excitement and happiness on her friend's face. "I am so pleased that he is agreeable. You have liked so many very *disagreeable* men."

Charlotte snorted. "Come, tell me more of what he said at the dance," Emilia insisted, hoping that her friend's happiness might somehow erode the influence of the duke's unpleasant family.

CHAPTER EIGHT

In the darkness of the billiard room, heavy shadows had formed as the men smoked and drank together.

Adam stood at the side with Lionel, watching Lord Sternwood and Lord Pinkerton play. Pinkerton was by far the worse for drink between the two and almost scratched the table with his cue on his third attempt to strike the ball.

Adam had noticed Frederick hovering behind him, but it was only when Lionel stepped away to refresh his drink that Frederick finally approached him.

"It has been a few months since I saw you, cousin," Frederick said with a smile. Adam had deliberately distanced himself from that side of the family, but he noted the familiarity Frederick tried to inject into his tone.

"I hope your mother is doing better," he offered.

"She is; thank you for the flowers you sent. I owe you an apology, nonetheless, as I was unable to attend Anastasia's funeral. My mother's health was much afflicted at the time as well."

A lead weight landed in the pit of Adam's stomach. He had been happily thinking of Lady Emilia up until that point, but Frederick's words destroyed any anticipation he might have felt at seeing her again.

His aunt and Lionel rarely spoke of Anastasia; they knew the effect it had on him, but Frederick seemed to have no such compunction. His voice would have sounded remorseful to anyone else, but Adam knew better. Nothing that Frederick said was sincere unless it related to himself.

"Thank you," Adam said stiffly. "You wrote me a letter at the time. I understood well enough."

Frederick sipped his drink, observing his cousin with interest. The man had become ghostly pale at the mention of his wife. *Perhaps ensuring he remains unattached will be easier than I thought.*

If Adam's response to the mere mention of his wife's name caused this type of reaction, Frederick could only imagine what would happen if he accused him of showing attention to another.

"She was a wonderful woman and a great credit to you. I am glad to see you out and socialising again after so long." Adam's response was only to swallow, his jaw visibly tightening.

"Bentley!" Both men turned at the call, neither of them certain who was being hailed. "Will you play?" Lord Sternwood asked, looking at Frederick.

Frederick felt a shudder of nerves. He could not afford to play deep tonight; he had barely a coin to his name after an ill-advised trip to a gambling hell. But he could hardly refuse his host.

"Of course, my Lord, prepare to be trounced!" Every man in the room laughed heartily except for Adam, and Frederick bowed to him and made his way over to the table.

Lionel cursed inwardly as he returned with their drinks to find Frederick walking away from his cousin. Adam looked deathly pale, and Lionel could only imagine what the blaggard had said to him.

"Here, old chap," he said, handing the small quarter inch of whisky to him. "Barely a thimble full, as requested."

Adam's smile was genuine as he received the glass, and they touched the tips together in a gentle clink.

"Thank you," Adam murmured, sipping his drink and watching Frederick's back as he bent over the billiard table. All the ease and happiness Lionel had felt in Miss Fairfax's company drained away as the melancholy returned to Adam's face.

"Anything amiss?"

Adam grunted. "He was speaking of Anastasia's funeral."

Lionel scoffed. "Yes, he was with his *mother*. That's what he told you, is it?"

"Yes. I had rather hoped it was a rare truth, but from your expression, I assume I am mistaken?"

"He was on the continent, I'm afraid. Wouldn't have made the trip back for anything. Too busy squandering his father's fortune all over France."

Lionel kept his voice carefully low so they were the only two privy to his comments but the anger in it was palpable.

"Gentlemen," the murmurings and chatter of the room died away as Lord Sternwood stood back from the billiard table as the clock chimed. "I am afraid the time has run away with me. I have my orders from Lady Sternwood that we must all return to the drawing room at this time. Please, make your way back to the other room. Mr Frederick, I shall see if you can *trounce* me another time."

***

Lady Sternwood was standing at the head of the room as the men all filtered back inside. She frowned at her husband, who was still smoking his cigar, and he dutifully stubbed it out before taking his seat.

The room was now inhabited by everyone who would be staying for the house party over the next two weeks. The group was twenty in number, comprising the Fairfaxes, Sterlings, and Pinkertons. Frederick and his mother, as well as Adam's direct family, made up the rest, along with the Cheswick's and the Duke's family.

It was a lively group, and Adam was gratified that many of the company were at least well-known to him. Perhaps the next few days would not be so arduous after all.

"We will be playing charades gentlemen and as the rest of the guests have departed, we will be splitting everyone into pairs."

In front of Lady Sternwood was an exquisitely decorated red and green bowl with names placed inside. Snow fell in a great curtain behind the long windows, and the room had an ethereal and beautifully festive feel.

Adam waited for the usual discomfort to arrive, never entirely comfortable in such a festive setting. Yet as his gaze landed on Emilia Sterling, the feeling never came. She was seated beside Miss Fairfax, looking rather stern but just as beautiful as ever, and he found that he could not look away.

"Lord Bellebrook," Lady Sternwood announced as the first name was picked. "And Lady Emilia Sterling!"

With nerves churning in his gut, Adam walked over to his new partner, overjoyed to find that she had a space next to her on the settee. He sat, with a smile, elated to be so close to her again as the other names were read out.

"Are you good at charades, my Lord?" Emilia asked, surprising him.

"I have not played before," he confessed.

"Not even when you were a child?" she asked, astonished.

"Ah, well, yes, but I always played with Lord Spencer, and he is a demon at every game. He wins everything. I do not know if I am good or bad, considering that I was never given the opportunity to win."

Emilia chuckled. "Well, we shall find out today. It is not only a game of riddles but also a game of wit to *guess* the riddle."

"Are you good at charades, Lady Emilia?" he asked in turn.

Emilia gave him a conspiratorial look, the same charming smile on her face that he had seen at the dinner table. "I would not wish to boast," she said quietly, "but I have been told my skills rival my musical talents."

"We will certainly win, then. I am very happy to be paired with you."

The comment was meant casually, but as her eyes met his, something passed between them of shared understanding. He *was* pleased to be paired with her. Despite all of the guilt and uncertainty that came with the idea of courting again, he enjoyed her company and could not think of anyone else he would rather spend time with at that moment.

The first riddle was read by Lord Sternwood, who begrudgingly yielded to his wife's insistence to commence the game. Emilia stifled a laugh as Lady Sternwood pushed her husband to the front of the room.

"I am a creature swift and bright,
In polished homes, I gleam at night.
I warm the heart and light the way,
Yet flicker out at break of day.
What am I?"

"A candle!"

Adam stared at Emilia in amazement, and she grinned at him. The expression utterly transformed her face, and he found himself captivated by it. He laughed as there were prolonged groans from everyone else in the room.

"You must give people a chance to *think*, my love," her mother admonished her.

"My apologies, Mama, but I will not delay my guessing for another to snatch the win."

Lady Sternwood rolled her eyes but said nothing more, and Adam had to hide his own smile.

Emilia placed her hands in her lap and watched the game continue, feeling a little on edge. She wasn't sure if she should hold back and allow others to guess more quickly, but she wanted to impress Lord Bellebrook. The feeling was so strong it had startled her but she had not considered what he might think of her competitive side. She hoped he would be thankful for it, given that he was part of her pair.

As the other riddles were read, each one became progressively more difficult. Lord Bellebrook's head was repeatedly bowed toward her as they considered their answers, their voices whispering intimately together.

Yet even with the innocent nature of the game, Emilia was acutely aware of how precarious her situation was. She could not afford to outwardly give the wrong impression or hint at her interest in the earl.

She ensured that there was always a reasonable distance between them, constantly flicking glances across the room, aware of the duke's presence and the continual scrutiny of society.

She had believed the feelings stirring within her long buried. Resigned as she was to a life of spinsterhood, she had not expected to meet anyone at the party that was to her liking. The only thing of which she was certain, however, was that the duke was *not*.

Lord Bellebrook had an interesting face. Where his cousin was dark in his features and looked many years younger than Lord Bellebrook, the earl was rugged and devilishly handsome. She rather felt he wore it with unknown grace and seemed oblivious to his own charms.

She glanced at him furtively throughout the evening, and the more she observed him, the more she liked what she saw.

The next riddle had the theme of cold, and he turned to her with his head cocked to one side.

"*My first is a posture, unmoving and still,*" Adam whispered. His head was lowered to hers again and she felt the heat of his body as she leaned toward him.

"A statue, perhaps?" she asked.

"Indeed, that was my feeling, and then '*my second you might see on stage in a play'.*"

There was a short pause as they deliberated and then they both looked up in enthusiastic surprise, and Emilia saw him grin for the first time. It caught her breath, and for a moment, she could not speak.

"Unmoving and still—perhaps to stall!"

"And then the second verse was 'caverns of ice'."

"Stalactite!" they both said it at once, far louder than they had intended, in mutual excitement. As Lady Sternwood bowed her head to let them know their answer was correct, Emilia was thrilled to find that they had won the game.

Frederick watched Adam and Emilia together and clapped along with the rest of the room as their answer was announced as the right one. He could feel sweat on his forehead at the sight of the two of them. *Thick as thieves already.*

He swallowed around the lump that threatened to rise in his throat. It was ridiculous that his miserable hermit of a cousin had found an attachment within hours of attending the only social function he had been to in years.

Frederick leaned across to converse with Lady Pinkerton beside him, keeping up appearances and speaking of how *very good* Lord Bellebrook and Lady Emilia were as a pair.

He would not be able to allow this to continue. His thoughts at the ball had been preliminary at best, but now he realised that their connection was a true possibility. Anyone with half a wit could see how much they enjoyed each other's company. They were minutes from finishing each other's sentences—it was utterly intolerable.

Frederick kept his smile in place, even yelling out 'bravo' to the company to ensure he looked as enthusiastic as possible. He would find a way to drive a wedge between them—he had to. There was no alternative. He could not afford to lose the fortune he deserved, and by God, Emilia Sterling was not going to take it from him.

***

Emilia's eyes skittered around the room uncertainly as the applause rang out all around them. There were many polite smiles in the throng, but when her gaze alighted on Penelope Easton, all her happiness drained away. Penelope's look was just like the one she had seen from Henrietta all those years ago.

She moved away from Lord Bellebrook, suddenly painfully aware of how close they had become. It was like she was living the nightmare of the scandal for a second time—she could already imagine the gossip spreading. *"She could not get her hooks into a married man, so she has set her sights on a wealthy widower".*

As Adam turned to her, his blue-green eyes sparking with gentle happiness, she managed a smile but moved further from him on the settee, glancing about the room in alarm, wondering if she had exposed herself again. The ice that rushed through her stomach at the thought was an awful reminder of everything she had been through.

She attempted to remain civil and courteous, but the mood between them changed considerably as the game wound down.

Adam watched Emilia with concern, wondering if he had somehow offended her. She seemed reserved suddenly, as she had been when they had first met. There was a strange detachment in her gaze, that looked deliberate, yet sad. As the game concluded and the group dispersed, she bid him goodnight, thanking him for the game. He longed to accompany her out of the room but held himself back.

He watched her walk away, wondering in a strange turn of events what Anastasia would have made of her. He believed they would have got along well. Anastasia was of the same quiet nature. He could no longer deny that despite the guilt he felt at looking at another woman with any kind of interest, he liked Lady Emilia Sterling very much.

She was witty, clever, and fiercely talented. Unlike many other women of his acquaintance, she was demure and sensible. As he made his way up to his room, Adam felt a warmth of affection toward her—terrifying and wonderful in equal measure.

As Emilia closed the door of her bed chamber, she breathed a sigh of relief, sliding down the wood to the floor and sitting on the thick carpet, allowing herself a moment of quiet contemplation. She could not believe all that had taken place.

The duke had been insufferable and drunk for much of the evening, not to mention his horrible daughters had put her in her place multiple times. But she had come away from what should have been an acute humiliation with lightness in her heart—all because of Lord Bellebrook.

The connection between them felt as fine as a strand of gossamer, loosely linking them to one another, but primed to break at the slightest pressure. She did not know what lay in her future, but the only easy decision she could make was that she must avoid the duke at all costs.

CHAPTER NINE

The following morning, Emilia had risen with the dawn's first light.

She had spent several hours watching the ghostly, twisting snowflakes falling past her window in the darkness, her mind a maelstrom of thoughts giving way to unpleasant dreams.

When she finally got out of bed, the crackling of the fire greeted her ears, accompanied by the warm, enticing scent of cinnamon wafting from the kitchens below. There was a thick blanket of snow on the ground outside and a significant layer upon her window ledge. She pulled up the sash, smiling at the sparkling diamonds before her. She thought of collecting a small amount and throwing it down to the gardens, but she did not wish to disturb it.

Everything around the grounds was perfect, clean, and dazzlingly white. It appeared that a badger had trundled through the snow, leaving lumbering uneven footsteps below her, and she could see the evidence of birds having hopped about the flowerbeds.

She allowed herself the time to bask in the Christmas feeling of the season. The view from her window unfolded like a winter painting, frozen in time and unspoiled.

As she went down the stairs to the dining hall, a bustle of servants surrounded her. Many of them nodded in greeting, and she smiled at them in return, but her hands were plucking incessantly at her gown. She wondered whether, by the end of the week, she might have worn a hole through everyone.

The doors to the dining hall had been left open, the remaining guests helping themselves to breakfast. Emilia was grateful to take the opportunity to linger a little and not have to take a seat immediately. All of the Eastons had already arrived, and Penelope, Caroline, and Sophia were seated together, speaking in low voices.

The duke and his daughters were the most well-to-do of those who had remained. Emilia marvelled at how her mother could cope with twenty people all at once so close to Christmas, but as Lady Sternwood swept into the room, directing servants left, right, and centre, it appeared she was in her element.

As Emilia pondered what she wanted to eat for breakfast, someone cleared their throat behind her, and she tensed, expecting the duke. When she turned, however, it was to see her father standing rather awkwardly behind her.

"Are you alright, my dear?" he asked in an uncharacteristic show of affection. "You look pale."

"I did not sleep all that well," she remarked quickly. The last thing she needed was for her parents to worry about her to an even greater degree. "Are you alright, Papa? Have you enjoyed the party thus far?"

"Indeed I have; Bentley is a demon at cards, though. I had no idea the man played so deep."

Emilia felt a gnawing sensation in her stomach. "Lord Adam Bentley is a gambler?"

Her father raised his eyebrows in apparent disinterest. "Hardly. But Frederick Bentley, on the other hand, most certainly is. I lost a handful to him late into the night, foolishness of the highest degree. Best keep that from your mother, if you would."

He harrumphed good-naturedly and went to find his seat. Emilia could not hold back a chuckle. It was nice to be confided in by her father. Even though the circumstances of her union to the duke were not what she would ever have chosen, she had to admit that her parents were more relaxed this week than she had seen them in years.

An unpleasant sensation filled her at that thought. It was all very well for them to be relaxed because of her potential marriage, but they did not seem to care what her life would be like once it had happened. She looked over at the duke's daughters and decided to try to get to know them today. They could not be all bad.

She went to take a seat opposite them and attempted a smile at Penelope. The girl gave her a long, baleful glare, and then all three of them turned away and began to speak amongst themselves.

It was a slight and not a subtle one.

Emilia pursed her lips, glancing about, noticing Mrs Verity Bentley watching them. Emilia quickly looked away, picking up her teacup to distract herself. She felt her cheeks flame as the cup clattered against the saucer.

As she sat watching the duke's daughter deliberately avoid eye contact with her, the door opened, and her fingers clutched at the handle of her teacup even tighter as the other object of her thoughts walked into the room.

Adam Bentley looked impossibly good in a dark green waistcoat that perfectly enhanced the colour of his eyes. Despite breakfast usually being a more casual affair, he wore a neat cravat, and it looked as though his valet had cut his hair since the night before—he looked dashing, untouchable, and unfairly handsome.

Adam surveyed the room, feeling rather proud that he did not run screaming in the other direction. This house party was causing him to feel a continual jolt of nerves every time he came into a room. He tried to convince himself it was because of his lack of social experience recently, but he knew, in reality, it was the young lady in the centre of the table that was the cause.

Emilia's hair was tied back in a simple ribbon today, a burnt orange colour to match her dress. Adam cleared his throat several times when he realised he had followed the ribbon all the way down her neck and over her shoulder twice.

Forcing his gaze away, his eyes fell on his aunt, who was sitting beside Lionel. Augusta looked at Adam pointedly and glanced at Lady Seraphina, who had just taken a seat beside Emilia. Adam clenched his jaw, feeling the weight of expectation settle on his shoulders.

He stoically went to the edge of the room to get his breakfast and determined to try and say as little as possible, unless Lady Emilia happened to speak with him.

From the opposite side of the table, Lionel buttered his toast and watched his cousin out of the corner of his eye. He knew his mother was trying to foist Adam onto Lady Seraphina and hoped that his cousin would take the initiative and sit at the other end of the table.

But he found himself distracted from his irritation with his mother when Miss Fairfax joined them, sitting opposite him with a demure smile.

To his delight, Miss Fairfax handed him a small leather-bound book.

"What is this?" he asked, enchanted to receive a gift from her.

"It is not mine," Miss Fairfax said, her full lips curving in an apologetic smile. "I asked Emilia if she would mind lending it to me some weeks ago and I had intended to return it. However, before I do so, I wondered if you had read it?"

Lionel scanned the cover, noting the works of John Keats.

"I have not. Is it poetry?" he asked.

"It is. Some of the best I have read."

"I thank you;" he said, examining the spine, "it is a very slim volume."

"Keats has only published a few works so far, but I dearly hope he will do more. Emilia and I have been reading them together. It's better than Blake."

"Scandal!" Lionel said with mock outrage, and Miss Fairfax laughed prettily as she poured herself some tea.

"Pray, read it and tell me what you make of it," she said.

"I should very much like to do the same," Lionel's mother piped up beside him. "I have been told of Keats myself, although the teller felt he was rather overblown and decidedly odd."

"All the best poets are, Mama," Lionel said teasingly and caught Miss Fairfax's eye as he did so. He felt a violent jolt of desire in his chest as she smiled and looked down at her plate.

She was by far the loveliest thing he had ever seen. He had never been given a gift by anyone but his mother before and wished it were for him to keep. He had a foolish notion he would have it in his inner pocket, keeping the thought of her close to him all day.

Charlotte was thrilled as she watched the emotions bloom across Lord Spencer's face. The night before, she had asked Emilia rather reluctantly if she might continue lending the volume a while longer. Unfortunately, their friendship was such that Emilia teased her relentlessly when she found out who she wished to lend it to. Charlotte felt that the cat was rather out of the bag when it came to her affection for Lord Spencer. Emilia was not stupid enough to believe she did not admire him.

"Lionel, you will read that book away from the table!" Augusta said suddenly, and Lionel bowed his head like a penitent child and put the book in his pocket.

As he did so, however, he caught Charlotte's eye, and their gazes held for a long moment that seemed to stretch endlessly. As he kept looking at her, he smiled gently and patted his pocket. It was a tiny gesture, something no one else in the room would have seen, but it was a silent acknowledgement that he treasured her gift and would keep it close to him.

Charlotte barely tasted the food on her plate for the rest of the breakfast, her heart swelling to such a degree she could barely keep her own happiness from spilling out into the room.

After breakfast, the ladies returned to the drawing room to make Christmas wreaths.

It was a beautiful spread that Emilia had not seen for some time. Her mother appeared to have brought the entire garden into the little room, and the air was filled with the smell of pine and fir trees.

Many of the ladies present were so excited by the prospect of all this greenery that it took quite some time to get everybody seated. When she did manage to take her seat beside Charlotte, however, Emilia was distracted and could not manage her own wreath well at all.

The ivy and the holly that she was trying to place in a pleasing pattern about the laurel were sticking out at odd angles, and she could not get it to sit right. Charlotte, on the other hand, who was usually very bad at anything creative, had excelled herself. Her wreath was beautiful and perfectly proportioned.

"Are you alright, Emilia?" Charlotte asked. "Ignore them all if you can. They are wicked things."

Emilia, who had just pricked her finger violently on a holly leaf, glanced at her in confusion. But it was abundantly clear to whom she referred as the giggling that had been on the edge of her hearing rose in volume as the duke's three daughters leaned together at their table.

One of them appeared to be mimicking Emilia's wreath by pushing haphazard pieces of foliage into her own, at which point they would all shriek with laughter.

Emilia's resolve to try to get along with them was fading more quickly by the second. She knew nothing of their mother, save that she had seemingly failed to instil any civility or kindness in her children. In her mind, their father must be just as bad.

"Perhaps we should ask Papa to cancel Christmas," Caroline was saying, her face twisted into a sneer. "We would be evicted from our townhouse with such a monstrosity."

Emilia lowered her wreath to her lap and was mortified to find her lip trembling. Charlotte's comforting hand came over her own and lifted the wreath away from her for a few minutes as she attempted to improve it.

Emilia took the time to compose herself, and when she looked back, Charlotte had transformed it, somehow allowing the ribbon to make all of the disorder look deliberate.

"Your skill is nothing short of magical," Emilia said in a low voice, and Charlotte laughed, holding it up rather pointedly.

"Yours is far more unique than the others," Charlotte said loudly. "I do grow so tired of these uniform wreaths that all look the same at this time of year."

Emilia frowned at her but then glanced at Sophia Easton's table. All of the sisters had made identical, perfect-looking wreaths, as though they had been purchased from a florist. Emilia hid her smile, glancing gratefully at her friend.

***

Across the house in the saloon, all of the men had congregated to play cards.

Adam was losing every hand and finding himself growing more and more frustrated as things progressed.

"You seem distracted," Lionel murmured, as Adam groaned as he lost another hand. On the other side of the room, Frederick appeared to be winning everything, and Adam's gut clenched at the likelihood that his wayward cousin would be able to pay his vowels if he were called up.

"Bentley?"

Adam knew he was being horribly rude to his faithful friend, but he could not shake the distraction. In his mind's eye, two women's faces were entwined together, both Lady Emilia's and Anastasia's. He could not reconcile the two or drag them apart, and in the background was his mother's stoic form, all confusion at his indecision and betrayal of them all.

He felt as though he were not honouring Anastasia's memory with his feelings toward Emilia, yet the alternative was unthinkable—that she might set her cap at another and be lost to him forever seemed even worse, somehow.

A sense of loathing and jealousy toward the duke washed over him, leaving Adam feeling like a stranger in his own skin. The whole thing was driving him to distraction, and he could not even *see* the cards in his hand anymore, let alone play them.

Lionel frowned at his cousin. Adam was glaring at the table with such a furious expression that their game partners were giving him strange looks, and Lionel nudged him pointedly with his foot, but it did no good.

"Bentley," he hissed, and finally, Adam turned back to him.

"Yes," he said curtly. "My apologies. Is it my turn?"

The other two men at their table excused themselves, clearly growing tired of playing against two men who were so distracted. Lionel raised his eyebrows at Adam.

"What troubles you? Care to confide?"

"There is nothing to confide," Adam snapped, casting his cards onto the table. With a heavy sigh, he scrubbed a hand over his face and rose abruptly, walking away and out of the room altogether.

Lionel watched him with a sad hopelessness in his heart. He laid his own cards down and looked out of the large window beside him where the snow had begun to fall again. The curtain pulls had been tied with pieces of holly, and the bright red berries looked very cheerful against the scene.

He smiled to himself, a sense of contentment and satisfaction rolling through him that surprised him. It was strange to acknowledge that his cousin appeared to be in the most miserable state of his life when Lionel felt as though he were the happiest he had ever been.

His hand moved to his pocket, sliding inside and gripping the book Miss Fairfax had given him. Without anyone else to play cards just at that moment, Lionel drew out the book, sitting beside the window, reading the words of John Keats against a backdrop of virgin snow and utterly content with the world.

CHAPTER TEN

As the afternoon arrived, the guests gathered for tea.

Emilia entered with Charlotte only to be confronted by the duke's daughters assembled in a line as though they had planned it in advance.

They all looked her over in their usual manner, and Emilia felt Charlotte's hand tighten on her arm. They were standing just beyond the door, and it would be rude for her not to address them. She knew she could expect only a rebuke in return, but nevertheless, she had been brought up to be a polite young lady.

"Good afternoon," Emilia said to Sophia.

"Oh, good afternoon, Lady Emilia," she said in an ingratiating tone. "Your mother has truly outdone herself with this room. Caroline and I were just remarking upon it."

"Thank you."

"It is quite like a small box room in our home at the estate. Very quaint."

Sophia kept her voice just low enough for the rest of the company not to hear it. But Charlotte heard it, and Emilia quickly pulled her away before she could respond.

"She is utterly insufferable," Charlotte exclaimed as Emilia pushed her gently into a chair.

"Pray, do not create a stir," Emilia pleaded. "That would be the last thing we need after everything."

"Of course, I shan't cause a stir," Charlotte replied, narrowing her eyes at the three women who sat down not too far from them. "Though perhaps I shall put salt in her tea, instead."

Their conversation was cut short as Emilia's mother sailed into the room, greeting her guests happily. The Pinkertons had gone for a walk with Lady Seraphina's parents, but the remaining occupants of the room were lively and eager for the activity of the afternoon.

"I thought it might be good fun to share your stories of Christmas traditions today!" Lady Sternwood proclaimed.

Adam, who had just taken his seat behind those already settled, held back a groan, his worst nightmare becoming a reality.

Everyone who cared for traditions in my life is dead, he thought miserably. *Unless sitting alone in my study, drinking whisky is a tradition.*

"I would happily begin the game," the duke piped up, and Adam watched him pompously plump up his chest.

On second thoughts, maybe I shall invent a few, he thought with determination.

"As you know, my late wife was a lover of Christmas," the duke said loudly as his daughters nodded enthusiastically. "I have many traditions I could choose from."

He pretended to think, stroking his beard dramatically, and Emilia heard Charlotte tut beside her as he clicked his fingers as though in remembrance.

"The Yule Log!" he cried suddenly, and Penelope clapped her hands.

"Oh Mama, always brought in the largest yule log in the country," she exclaimed. "She decked it with the most beautiful greenery. It would burn for days."

"Quite right," the duke added testily, giving his daughter a warning glare. Penelope was silenced by it immediately. "The yule log was Hilary's favourite part of Christmas," his eyes shifted to Emilia's, "the hearths in the estate are so vast she could afford to have two burning at once." He nodded at the company. "She was a very charitable woman and always would invite members of the church congregation to tea to sit about and admire it."

"How wonderful!" Lady Sternwood said. To Emilia's mind, her enthusiasm was entirely misplaced, but her mother was looking at the duke as though he could spin gold. Emilia had to be careful to keep the irritation from her expression.

"I am told," the duke continued, "that Lady Emilia is a great lover of Christmas and has often made some quite beautiful decorations in this very house!"

Emilia shrank away as many eyes turned to her, and several people clapped even as Sophia Easton scoffed loudly.

"Oh, my daughter is talented at many things," Lady Sternwood added, looking proudly down at Emilia.

Adam observed the mother and daughter from the back of the room, conscious that Lady Sternwood's gaze appeared overly affectionate, even false, as though affected for the duke's benefit. His fists clenched in his lap, and he glanced warily at Emilia, watching the flush rise up her neck.

"Why, Emilia, you should play for us all," Lady Sternwood said swiftly.

There was much enthusiasm for that idea, and, given no choice, Emilia rose and walked slowly to the piano.

If my mother gets her way, I will be married to him before Christmas Eve, she thought bitterly.

Adam took the opportunity to examine the duke. He was not unattractive, with a square jawline and amicable expression, but his eyes were shrewd. Adam had barely had a chance to get to know Lady Emilia, but even he could see that they were total opposites. She was creative and gifted, whereas Adam had met enough businessmen to understand that the duke had a fortune for a reason—he likely kept his money close; many men like him were known to be spendthrifts.

Adam looked at the Elderbridge girls. They were all pretty enough but haughty and sneering. He had seen how they had treated Emilia at the ball and had overheard more than one unkind comment from them—not to mention their behaviour at the breakfast table.

No, that was not a family he would want to get to know in more intimate terms. A wave of protectiveness engulfed him again as he looked back at Emilia. She was all soft lines and intelligence. The Elderbridge's seemed tightly wound, like a spring ready to burst. He could not think of a worse match and looked over at Lord and Lady Sternwood, his teeth grinding together that they would allow it.

Emilia was now seated at the piano, and Adam felt a burst of anticipation as he waited for what she would play. It was clear that she had memorised more music than he had ever *heard* in his life, and his hands rubbed absently at the edges of his chair, waiting for the first notes. He caught Lionel's eye, who was watching him curiously, and Adam affected a more relaxed air, leaning back in his chair.

As the music began, however, his eyes closed as if guided by some unseen force. It was Handel's Passacaglia in G Minor. Recognising the piece she had chosen sent a wave of pride through him. He listened to it and let the music wrap around him, quite conscious that the rest of the company was not as enthralled as he. Some of them were even talking over the music, and he gripped the handle of his chair to prevent him from telling them to be quiet.

After about half a minute, however, the entire room fell silent. The music swelled through them like a tide, touching each person as it progressed.

In Adam's breast, something stirred. It was a feeling of unique ecstasy, a lightness that stretched from his sternum to the top of his head and fluttered there happily like a bird. If he could have described it, it felt like a straight line of shimmering gold that gently unfurled within him and expanded through his entire being.

His heart beat in tandem with the music, his back against the chair felt more vivid, his breath easier. Everything that was painful in his mind seemed to float away as though it had never been there, and for the longest moment, there was only Emilia and the music.

Emilia.

The piece ended, and Adam snapped back to the room as the applause began. He opened his eyes without any real understanding of where he was for a few seconds, but instantly, as though guided by a magnet, they found Emilia's.

She was watching him as though assessing what he might have thought of the piece. Adam quickly began clapping along with the rest of the room. When he should have looked away, however, he did not, and neither did she.

Their gazes locked, suspended like the final note of a high soprano, lingering in the air, gentle and soon to break. It faded and she looked away, but as the hubbub of the room returned, Adam could not hear it.

All he could hear was that single suspended chord, scattered with gold and diving inexorably down into his chest, straight to his heart.

***

The following day was grey and cold. The snow had continued to fall, and there were some grumblings in the house about how deep it was becoming. Many were concerned about the state of the roads, and the Marquess and Marchioness were not the only members of the party to speak of how grateful they were that they would not have to make a long journey until after Christmas.

The party had gathered to make Christmas baskets for the poor. Emilia, who had been asked to help her mother, carried the empty baskets into the room and handed them out to everyone.

Lionel Spencer and Lord Bellebrook were seated at one table, and Charlotte was close by, waiting for Emilia to sit beside her.

"It is rather hot beside the fire, is it not?" Lord Spencer commented as Emilia handed him a basket.

"Are you uncomfortable, my Lord?" she asked. "Perhaps we could move the table a little further away."

"Lionel, whatever are you about? We are a full five feet from it," Adam said, his eyes sparkling with amusement. However, the amusement quickly died when Lionel rolled his eyes at him.

"You never feel the heat, my friend, and are always chilled to the bone. I run hot and I cannot sit here another minute. Lady Emilia, would you be very cross if I moved to Miss Fairfax's table if you will permit me, Miss Fairfax."

Emilia held back a laugh at the artless way Lord Spencer was inserting himself into Charlotte's life, but a part of her rejoiced at the sight of it, too.

"As long as Lord Bellebrook does not mind a change in partners, I would not mind you doing so," she said. As she handed out the last of the baskets to Lady Pinkerton—who had no such qualms about the fire as was almost sitting inside the hearth—Emilia took her seat beside Adam, her hands trembling.

Upon the table were an array of various items, all of which warmed Emilia's heart. Her parents were by no means troubled by money, but her mother had been very generous, considering how many boxes they would make with almost twenty guests.

The items that were scattered before her were delicate tartan fabrics curled into rolls and tied with sprigs of holly. There were small fabric sacks that contained woollen socks and some finer strips of cloth dotted amongst them. Their cook had prepared several dozen pots of jam and preserves that had been laid out across the tables—they were Emilia's father's favourite, and she was touched that he would wish to use them in this way.

Adam was surveying the table with a look of confusion.

"I do not believe I would know where to begin. All of the ladies have made everything look so beautiful. I am afraid I am not good at creative pursuits," he said, fingering one of the candles that was laid at the side of the table and almost knocking it to the floor.

Emilia struggled to settle her nerves being so close to him again and was conscious that she had been staring at his face for far too long for it to be natural. She looked hurriedly back at the table and nodded.

"I felt the same when I began making the baskets, but there is no right way to do it. Everything in them will be of some use to a family in need and they will not care how they are presented, just that they are received."

Adam visibly relaxed at her words, and a little smile played over his lips as he leaned forward. He stretched his long legs beneath the table, and Emilia felt a little thrill as they brushed against the edge of her skirts.

"You did not speak of your traditions, Lady Emilia. Is this one, perhaps?" Adam asked.

"Oh yes," Emilia replied, thinking of the Cartwright family in the village. Their father had been badly injured in a farming accident, and her parents had been helping him manage the tenancy of his property in the hopes that he would recover. "I have given the baskets to the poor every holiday. Easter is my favourite, as they are so bright to look at. We paint eggs each year, and they are always well received."

"But Christmas, I suppose, has its charm too," Adam conceded, but his face did something strange that Emilia could not read. Something about the expression reminded her of the first time she had seen him, the vulnerability that seemed to be shared between them.

She was not sure what made her admit what she did next, but she expected it was that strange, unknown look at the back of his eyes.

"I have not enjoyed Christmas for many years," she confessed.

Adam, who was trying to place a candle in his basket and finding it too large, looked up at that and frowned at her.

"Really?" he asked, looking astonished. And then, more quietly. "I am the same."

Emilia breathed out, realising how grateful she was that he had not asked her *why* she did not like the festive season; he had just empathised with her feelings.

"I loved Christmas when I was a child," she added, "and it is usually a joyful time, but lately it has felt a little…"

"Hollow," he finished for her, and Emilia felt something loosen in her chest.

"Yes. Exactly. I think this year is the first where I have felt the seasonal joys I once did. It is, I am sure, having so many guests in the house and everything looking so festive."

"Do you know that Lord Spencer said the same to me before I came here? I confess that I was not sure if I should attend. I am not always the most jovial company at this time of year. But he was right. He told me I might feel Christmas cheer simply by being around others."

Those blue-green eyes found hers and there was such intensity within them that she was unable to look away.

"I have never been so grateful that he encouraged me to come."

Emilia pulled in a shallow breath as they both reached across the table to retrieve their items. Their fingers alighted upon the same object and an electric charge seemed to snap where their skin touched. Adam cleared his throat, moving his own hand away and giving her a nod as she took the item in question.

Emilia fought to conceal the fact that her hands were shaking violently.

Across the room, Lionel was watching his cousin with excitement bubbling in his chest. He had not seen Adam speak to anyone so intimately since Anastasia's death, and he had great hopes for the match.

"Miss Fairfax, you are quite outdoing yourself with your basket. You are making me look quite inept."

Charlotte looked at his rather forlorn offering and cocked her head to one side. "Isn't it dreadful?" he said with false melancholy. Charlotte's basket was beautiful and perfectly ordered. Even the colors were exactly as they should be, an array of reds, golds, and greens. It positively exuded Christmas. Somehow, Lionel had managed to make his own basket look entirely brown.

"It just needs some ribbon around the edges. Here, we shall swap, and I shall do a little tinkering with your basket if you allow me."

"Pray, take it away from me. I should sooner give it to a dog than to the poor. None of them would want it."

She laughed and began to wind a gold ribbon around the wicker at the edges without comment.

Charlotte was enjoying herself enormously. Lionel was already halfway through the book of poems and confessed to her that he had not been able to put it down until late into the night. His reaction had been similar to her own. He read the poems several times through and found new meaning in them every time he did.

Something about him reading the book she had suggested in his bed into the early hours sent a thrill of forbidden pleasure through her.

His basket was not so very bad, just a little haphazard in its style, and as she rectified it, she glanced at Emilia. Her friend and Lord Bellebrook were still talking in low voices with one another, Emilia no doubt conscious of keeping herself distant from him at all times.

Charlotte was very pleased to see her making a connection away from the influence of the duke. She wondered if she might devise an insult so appalling that the duke would leave the house in disgust. Smiling at the thought, she allowed herself to hope that something might blossom between Lord Bellebrook and Emilia.

"I have not seen Adam so open for many months," Lionel commented, surprising her as she turned to him. She raised her eyebrows as though she did not understand to what he referred, and he gave her a knowing smile that made him look even more handsome than he already was. "Christmas can be a trying time. I am simply glad he has ventured out of his study and found someone with whom he can converse who is not me or his aunt. We were growing very tired of him."

Charlotte really did laugh then, and as she presented his basket back to him, Lord Spencer exclaimed to no limited degree that she was a 'marvellous creature,' and she felt herself blush up to her hairline at the praise.

"Ladies and gentlemen," came Lord Sternwood's voice from the back of the room. "Spillikins!"

There were many exclamations from the group as the baskets were moved to the side in their completed state. Many seemed relieved that they would not have to make any more, and Lionel was very much among their number.

Emilia and Adam preceded them into the drawing room where Spillikins had been set up for them all to play. Lionel enjoyed the game but had not played it for some time.

A number of sticks had been poured onto a table where the guests all gathered. Lionel felt anticipation run through him as he brushed against Miss Fairfax, who was already looking at the game with an analytical eye.

"Shall we be a pair?" he asked innocently.

Lionel was many things, but he was not a coward. He had had some dalliances with women in the past, but he had never met anyone like Charlotte Fairfax. Increasingly he was beginning to think that he should make his intentions known. Life was too short, as his father would say, to let the chances slip by without grabbing them with both hands.

"Why yes!" Miss Fairfax replied and bent over the table as they strategised on the best stick to choose. The game was simple in its construction—each pair would try to remove a stick without jostling or dislodging any of the others. It was fiendishly difficult towards the end when the majority of the sticks were placed in the centre.

Emilia watched Charlotte and Lord Spencer work together, and although she was happy for her friend, she also felt a longing for simpler connections. She had greatly enjoyed her time with Lord Bellebrook, but there was no guarantee that anything more would exist between them once the party ended.

Perhaps it is enough that I should befriend him, she thought.

But the reality of her life loomed large beside her as the duke stepped up and took his turn. There would be nothing whatsoever between her and the earl if her parents got their way.

"Where would you suggest?" the duke asked her, and Emilia noticed many eyes turning to them.

"Why, your Grace, we are not a pair," she protested gently, terrified that simply pointing out the truth would begin a scandal of some kind. To her relief, however, the duke laughed.

"Quite right, quite right, I shall forge on alone."

The game became more and more competitive as it continued, and there was much laughter and enjoyment by all. Several of the party were eliminated, but to Frederick's irritation, as he stepped up as one of the final few, the *lovebirds* remained unbeaten. Adam was fawning over Emilia as though they were already engaged.

Frederick's hand shook as he removed his stick and there were shouts of dismay as he pulled it free holding it up in triumph. He watched Emilia and Adam lower their heads together and decide on which they would choose. His ire rising all the while Frederick wondered if he should simply jolt the table and end the game.

He was uncomfortable with how closely they were standing and the way Adam's eyes lingered on her for the longest time.

When Anastasia died, it should have guaranteed his ascendency, particularly with Adam barely leaving his rooms. Frederick had been sure the man would die of grief, and yet here he was, larger than life and making a new alliance.

Frederick glanced at the duke, who had clearly noticed the growing bond between them. The man's face was puce as he flicked his gaze back and forth between Emilia and Adam. There was nothing improper in how they behaved—Emilia would be far too careful for that.

But he could see the duke's displeasure—and that meant there was a way for his plan to begin.

CHAPTER ELEVEN

The following morning began with a church service at the manor's private chapel.

Emilia was struck by the party's opulence against the chapel's relatively drab appearance. There were rich velvets and brocades among the dresses that the ladies were wearing, mixed with the cold stone and dark wood of the church interior.

A beautiful stained-glass window at the rear of the aisle cast a kaleidoscope of coloured light over the congregation as they took their seats.

It was another grey day outside, and she could see her breath as she walked toward her parents. Her mother turned and glanced behind her pointedly, and Emilia's heart sank as she saw the duke and his daughters in the row behind.

The duke turned with a smile, gesturing for her to sit beside him. Emilia looked at her mother, but Lady Sternwood had already turned back to face the front of the chapel.

The stained glass along the wall was throwing patterns across the little congregation, and she did not think it was a coincidence that Benedict Easton was bathed in red from the light above him. It made him look rather demonic, and when she sat beside him, the stench of brandy was strong. It was still early in the morning; he must have already been drinking, or perhaps he had done so late into the night.

She swallowed back the nausea that the smell prompted and forced a polite smile.

"You are looking very well this morning," the duke said, running his eyes over her. Emilia was glad of her thick coat in the cold interior of the chapel, but there was something in the way the duke looked at her that made her feel naked in his presence. She hated being close to him. It did not help matters that Sophia was glaring daggers at her behind her father's back and Emilia looked away to hide her discomfort.

As she did so, the sight of Lord Bellebrook was a welcome one. He was wearing his own thick greatcoat and looked every bit as dashing as he had at the ball. The Earl of Bellebrook had the ability to appear far grander than someone like the Duke. It was almost as though Elderbridge affected his superiority, and Lord Bellebrook possessed it without even trying.

Adam sat on the opposite side of the church with his aunt and cousin. For a brief moment, he looked across at her as they all stood for the opening hymn. Emilia experienced a strange calm come over her at that look, which she could not explain. Something in having Adam close by was a balm to her fractured nerves. She did not know why he had such an effect on her, but she was grateful he was there.

As she began to sing, with Elderbridge's booming voice beside her, it was almost as though she could feel Adam's calming presence wrap around her, shielding her from the world, as though it was just the two of them.

"Do you think if I lit a candle to keep my hands warm anyone would notice?" Lionel asked and Adam gave him a warning glance. There were not enough people in the church to mask Lionel's voice during the hymn and he was aware of the Pinkerton's glaring at them irritably.

"I think the vicar would notice if you were to set the church on fire, yes."

"It is freezing in here," Lionel hissed, rubbing his hands against his thighs.

"Would you be still? You are making me feel colder."

Adam gripped his hymn book more tightly and forced his eyes ahead of him when all he wanted to do was look at Lady Emilia again. This morning, she was wearing a dark coat and a dark hat to match it, and she looked effortlessly elegant. His own gloved hands were chilled beneath the thick fabric, and he hoped she had enough layers on to keep her warm.

The chapel itself was beautiful and ornate, with gold leaves climbing up the lectern where the vicar stood. As the first hymn ended, he sat down, surprised by how at ease he felt. It might have been the setting, but the notes of worry he had felt ever since he had arrived at the manor seemed to have faded.

He had wed Anastasia in a small chapel much like this one. Neither of them had been interested in a grand occasion. It had been a wonderful day, and in his mind's eye, he was standing at the aisle with her, waiting for her to become his wife.

As the memory flooded his brain he looked to his left, anticipating Anastasia's familiar smile, but was instead met by Emilia's vibrant presence. Adam jolted sideways in his seat making his aunt gasp and she looked at him in consternation.

"My apologies," he murmured, his voice coming out as a croak.

What on earth has come over me?

Despite only knowing Emilia for two days, she had become thoroughly embedded in his mind and seemed to have permeated all of his senses. When he had woken that morning, she had been his first thought—not Anastasia, as he was accustomed to—but Emilia. He thought of her smile often, and each time he did so, it made him see her again.

That line of shimmering joy that had begun with her music was spreading like a flower blooming in his chest, and he seemed unable to stop it. The guilt he felt at Anastasia's memory was there and perhaps would always be, but somehow, the sharp edge to it had dulled. He felt hopeful for his future, the dark walls of his study and endless ledgers finally losing their appeal after all these years. He felt ready for a change.

How good it would be to fill the world with colour. Every time he was around Emilia, he felt as though everything was brighter and clearer.

Adam rose with the congregation, having no idea what had just been said as another hymn began. He glanced at Emilia, his hands tightening further on his book as he saw her take a subtle step away from the Duke of Elderbridge.

I cannot be mistaken; there is no interest there.

He kept his eyes on Emilia's elegant form throughout the service, her face bathed in golden light from the windows above her, and his heart feeling as though it was bathed in it, too. It was as though everything he had believed, all the light in his life that he had assumed was snuffed out, had merely been in the darkness, waiting for someone to draw it out again.

As they exited the chapel, the snow was still falling in earnest. It was so thick, and the day so cold, that the snowflakes were adhering to every surface, even vertical lampposts.

The ground about them was devoid of any path, despite it having been cleared just that morning. Adam was taken aback by the beauty of it, wishing he could stand and watch it fall for hours. The soft brush of each flake on the ground was soothing to his ears, and he pictured walking through it with Emilia by his side speaking of music and all the things she loved.

But the Sterlings seemed concerned by the snowstorm that had erupted about the guests and ushered everyone quickly back to the manor without any time for dallying.

Lionel and Adam stamped their feet as they entered the house, and tea was brought to the drawing room, where everyone was invited to assemble. Adam glanced at Lionel as his cousin helped him with his coat and scoffed quietly as he made a show of folding it and handing it to the butler with a bow.

"You are a simpleton," Adam muttered affectionately.

"The cold air suits you, cousin," Lionel replied. "You look better in the last few days than you have these past few years. I do hope you will continue to venture from the house. It makes you look rather less like an ogre."

Adam let out a bark of laughter at that and noticed Lady Seraphina Cheswick glance across at him with a demure smile as her parents fussed over her gown.

Adam gave her a short nod in response, unsure how he was to navigate the next few days. Lady Seraphina was not an unpleasant girl, but she paled in comparison to Lady Emilia. Lady Seraphina's mother clearly had designs upon his affections, and his own aunt had made it clear he needed to make an alliance.

Was he foolish to think Lady Emilia might become that alliance? After so short a time, the idea seemed like madness—but nevertheless, it persisted.

Emilia sat beside Charlotte in the drawing room as her mother and father debated what they should do due to the snow. They had been planning a walk that afternoon, but the heavy snowfall and the steep drop in temperature meant that their plans were thwarted.

"Emilia, we shall do a recital," her mother whispered to her as the other guests began to gather. "You will begin it, and then we will ask others to take their turn."

Emilia did not argue. Her mother had been taken aback by the depth of the snow and was obviously agitated. Lord Sternwood gave Emilia a reassuring nod as he handed her one of her favourite books of poetry, and Charlotte smiled.

"Excellent choice, Lord Sternwood," Charlotte remarked, having known Emilia's father for many years and feeling comfortable in his presence. "You have exquisite taste."

Emilia's father chuckled. He had always been very fond of Charlotte.

Emilia felt her palms sweating as she plucked at the edge of her dress. Charlotte was all smiles and encouragement as her audience settled themselves. Emilia was not a natural performer when a piano was not in front of her, and she felt nerves slice through her.

But as she looked across the room, she saw Lord Bellebrook opposite. Lionel Spencer seemed preoccupied with trying to catch Charlotte's eye, but Adam was looking at her—and only her. He gave her a small smile and a nod, and Emilia finally found the strength to rise and stand before the room.

She opened the book, glancing at Charlotte, who was now paying rapt attention and began to read. The poem was by Wordsworth and spoke of lost love and redemption. To Emilia, with Adam's eyes upon her, she felt as though it spoke for him of all he had lost and was yet to gain from life.

Adam watched Emilia, her full lips reciting and growing bolder as the poem continued. It was interesting to watch her speak like this. The pianoforte was a natural thing for her, almost an extension of herself, and in a recital she did not seem so comfortable.

He leaned forward, trying to instil in her his silent encouragement. He thought of all she had endured in the preceding years and the pain it must have caused her and her family to be so shunned by society.

He had heard a little more from Augusta on the subject, and it was true; there had been no evidence of what had happened with Lord Julian Blackmoor. The man himself had denied it on every occasion since, and yet for Emilia, the derision from those such as the duke's daughters was still palpable to this day.

Adam's fingers clenched at the injustice of it all. He found himself lost in her words as she continued, watching her mouth move around the stanzas, the poise in her figure, the lightness in her tone. Her confidence grew from the beginning to the end, the slight shake in her voice fading as she reached the conclusion.

With a sigh of relief, she lowered the book, and everyone began to clap in earnest. She glanced at him, as his heart kicked hard in his chest and a blush suffused her cheeks as she curtsied and sat down. Adam was captivated by her and had to drag his gaze away to focus on Charlotte Fairfax as she rose to read her poem.

Charlotte's reading was by Keats and Adam knew that Lionel had been touched by the gift of the poems from her. He glanced at his cousin to see what he thought of the reading, but Lionel only had eyes for Miss Fairfax.

Lionel's posture was just as Adam's had been as he had listened to Emilia. His cousin was leaning forward, his handsome face poised in deep concentration, his fists clenched so tightly Adam could see the whites of his knuckles.

"Wonderful," Lionel whispered breathlessly as the poem concluded and was the loudest in the applause by quite some way.

The two men looked at one another in that moment, and a wealth of emotion was passed between them without words. They looked back to Lady Emilia and Miss Fairfax sitting together after their readings, and both of them sat back in their chairs in tandem as though exhausted by it all.

"I am genuinely glad we came," Lionel said softly. Adam could only reply with a wan smile—he most heartily agreed.

As Charlotte settled beside her, Emilia squeezed her friend's hand and murmured her congratulations. Charlotte was adept at reading aloud and the ability came far more naturally for her. Even so, Emilia was always surprised by how much she enjoyed the aftermath of a challenging experience. Before every performance, she was always horribly nervous, yet the excitement at the end was always worth the fear.

As the recital ended, however, and the guests began to disperse. Elderbridge was at her side in a moment, and Emilia watched Charlotte give him a stiff glance before her friend reluctantly had to leave them alone.

"That recital was exquisite, my Lady," the duke said, leaning into her, his heavy bulk causing her to step lightly to the side as his torso almost brushed her arm. "You have a true passion in your words and a depth of feeling. I was quite moved."

"Thank you, your Grace."

"My daughters adore reading aloud, and we always have many occasions to do so at my estate. I would dearly love to hear you read again; I have never been so captivated."

Emilia smiled. "You are too kind."

Too kind and insincere. Emilia knew she had read without too many errors, but her cadence was often not quite as it should be when reading poetry—the emphasis on the words a little stilted. The duke was complimenting her to get into her good graces, and she did not appreciate it.

As Adam moved to leave the room, he noticed that the duke had cornered Emilia again. The man simply would not leave her alone and must have had the intelligence of a dullard to think she was encouraging him. He glanced at Lord and Lady Sternwood and realised that it did not matter. The duke did not *need* Emilia to want him, her parents approved and that was all that was required.

Adam clenched his jaw in irritation at the predicament Lady Emilia found herself in.

"You look positively murderous, Adam," his aunt said suddenly beside him and he glanced at her, schooling his features as best he could.

Her intelligent eyes moved to Emilia and back to him, and she hooked her arm in his pointedly steering him out of the room. As he looked back, the duke rested an arm on Emilia's elbow, and Adam had to force his feet to keep moving out of the door before he ran back and wrenched him away from her for good.

Perhaps there is a way that I can save her, he thought. *Perhaps there is a way that I can save us both.*

CHAPTER TWELVE

That evening her mother had arranged a small soiree in the ballroom. It would not be as grand as the first ball of the house party, but there were still some guests joining them for the evening which meant there would be some variety in those attending.

Emilia fussed with her gown as her maid put the finishing touches to her hair. Her mother had ordered her dress some weeks before for this very occasion and Emilia loved the look of it.

It was dark green in colour with a hint of purple in the train and it picked out the copper strands in her hair. As she descended the stairs, she stopped halfway down, noticing the duke hovering outside the ballroom. The remaining guests were already inside as newcomers began to draw up in their carriages in front of the doorway. Emilia could see Lionel and Charlotte laughing together just inside the room.

There was no reason for the duke to be waiting outside unless he had intended to speak with her. As soon as she took another step, he glanced up with a smile that did not quite reach his eyes and walked over to her.

"Ah, Lady Emilia, you are a vision," he said, putting her teeth on edge.

"Your Grace," she said and was forced to take his arm. Emilia tried to remain relaxed but could feel the tension growing in her shoulders.

"Let me get you a glass of punch; your mother has infused my soul with Christmas these last few days. I have never seen such beautiful and abundant decorations."

Somewhere in the compliment, there was a hint of reproof, but Emilia could not put her finger on what it might be. Many households did not decorate to the extent that her mother had done, but Lady Sternwood adored all things during the festive season, and Emilia was proud of her for all the work she had put into the ball.

They walked inside, Emilia feeling a pang of longing as she saw Adam across the floor. He was standing with his aunt, leaning in and whispering something in his ear. Adam's gaze was fixed on Lady Seraphina Cheswick on the other side of the room, and Emilia's heart clenched.

She would be a far more suitable match. She thought sadly. *No hint of scandal, and she is younger even than me.*

She wondered how old Lord Bellebrook's late wife had been and what sort of a woman she was.

"Here you are," the duke said, handing her a crystal glass. "Fruit cordial. I remember it is your favourite."

He had seen her drinking it once not two days before, and Emilia was finding it more and more difficult to retain the smile on her face.

"Pray tell me, your Grace, you have six daughters, is that correct?"

"Indeed I do. Bertha and Miriam have been married for some years. Eliza was married last June and lives not too far from here."

Emilia nodded but was increasingly aware of eyes moving toward them from around the room. Lady Pinkerton nodded to her with a beaming smile.

Everyone can see his intentions toward me when he stands beside me like this. This is torture!

"Would you do me the honour of a dance, my Lady?"

Cornered and unable to refuse, Emilia had no choice but to take his hand. She prayed that she might fall awkwardly and sprain her ankle, but the duke's arm was firm and confident against hers, keeping her well-supported.

As the duke led her to the floor, she saw Lord Spencer and Charlotte were at the other end of the line with Lord Bellebrook and Lady Seraphina making up another pairing.

Emilia's chest tightened horribly as she looked at Adam and Seraphina. All the hopes and fantasies she had entertained over the last few days seemed impossibly foolish now she saw him standing up with another. They made a very attractive pair.

As the dance began, Emilia noted that her mother had chosen a set that required no movements between partners. She, therefore, had to endure endless prattle from the duke about her accomplishments, how much he adored the pianoforte, and how his daughters had enjoyed it, too.

Thankfully, Sophia was the only one dancing and was some way from them. Emilia was spared her scoffs of disagreement as the duke told the bare-faced lie.

She was under no illusions that if she became their stepmother, she would have no more authority over them than a servant. Her feet faltered a little as she continued the steps, the room around her seeming to blur into a confusing mess of colours and sounds as the reality of what was happening lowered over her.

I am going to be promised to this man for the rest of my life because of a scandal in which I played no part and did nothing wrong.

The duke was looking at her oddly and she realised her fists were clenched tightly at her sides, and she had missed a part of the dance with him. She concentrated on the steps, and as the dance blissfully came to an end, she curtsied, yearning for the escape of the refreshment table.

To her horror, however, her father and mother immediately came toward her. She thought she might detect some sorrow in her father's expression for a few seconds, but it lifted almost as soon as it came.

The duke's daughters all came to stand with them, and the duke was so close to Emilia that she could smell the whisky on his breath. She kept her back taut, trying to retain her composure. Sophia was all smiles now, as were Caroline and Penelope. Emilia was taken aback by how affable they were.

"You are an excellent dancer, Lady Emilia," Sophia exclaimed, glancing at her father with a sharp smile. "I must say I greatly enjoyed your recital this afternoon."

The speech felt practised, as though she were reciting it herself. Emilia wondered if their father had scolded them for their coldness toward her; she would not be in the least surprised if that were the case.

"Thank you, your own recital was very well read. I do not have the aptitude for poetry that others do."

"But you make up for it with your skill on the piano." That was Caroline's voice. Of all his daughters, she seemed to be the one who followed the others rather than being actively hostile on purpose. If anything, she simply appeared bored.

"Lady Emilia has many accomplishments, as my girls have pointed out over the days we have spent here. Lord Sternwood, I compliment you on an excellent house party so far. I have never enjoyed so many diverting activities and with such excellent company."

Emilia's face was hot, her palms sweating profusely. The new dress suddenly felt tight and suffocating and she was alarmed to find that her vision was fading in and out of focus.

She could not bear it. This insufferable man and his terrible children were going to trap her into a life of misery. She would be surprised if there were even a piano in his house. Even if there were she could imagine him giving her permission to use it only when he saw fit. He did not seem the kind of man who took kindly to a woman exercising her intellect and choosing her own pursuits.

Emilia endured another ten minutes of talking before her mother suggested another dance. This time, the duke appeared to notice that he could not focus all his attention on Emilia so soon and asked Lady Seraphina instead.

"Mama, I am just going outside to get some air," Emilia said as carefully as she could. She expected her mother to insist that she remain, but to her surprise, Lady Sternwood turned to her with concern.

"Yes, my dear, you look very flushed. Are you alright?"

"Just a little tired from the dancing. This is such a beautiful evening, though, Mama. So many of the company have remarked upon it."

Her mother smiled in delight at the praise and rested a hand on her arm. "Do not stay outside too long. If you are flushed, you will not feel the cold, and it is bitter out there."

"I shall not. Thank you, Mama."

With overwhelming relief, she walked swiftly to the side of the ballroom and to the high doors that opened out onto the terrace.

Within seconds, she was outside in the freezing cold, shutting the door behind her and closing her eyes, trying to control the panic that was threatening to overwhelm her.

From the other side of the floor, Adam watched Emilia leave the room, frowning at her hurried footsteps. He had found his gaze constantly drawn to her throughout the dance. Seraphina had been far more tolerable, and he had been able to speak at least two sentences before she interrupted him this time, but he was aware he had barely listened to anything she had said.

Her parents were across the room speaking with her, and he could easily guess the subject of their conversation.

"It is an excellent match," Augusta said beside him for the fourth time. Adam shifted his weight, rolling his shoulders and trying to breathe steadily as his anger increased. His aunt was becoming desperate. The constant shadow of Frederick was clearly agitating her and her intimations had become more and more obvious as time drew on.

Frederick's presence had begun to creep into everything she did, and he could tell she was worried about his influence. Without an heir, the title would pass to Frederick without contest, and Adam and Augusta both knew how dangerous it would be for Frederick to get his hands on Adam's father's money.

Adam would happily have lent Frederick anything in the world if he could be trusted, but he had squandered his own fortune at an alarming rate.

Frederick had always been disingenuous and bitter. He saw himself as a victim, excluded unjustly from Adam's father's good graces. He knew how to speak well in company and had excellent breeding and manners to recommend him, but he had debts across the country that he was unable to pay, and Adam had no intention of opening his coffers to help him again.

If Frederick took over as the Earl of Bellebrook, the estate would be ruined in months, not years. He glanced at the door that Emilia had left through. There was an element of madness to the feelings that had crept through him in the days he had spent at this house, but one thing had remained steady—his regard and connection to her.

Thinking of her playing music stirred something deep within him. Watching her countenance and speaking with her of her hopes and dreams had given him a purpose in a way that he had not felt for a long time. He did not want Lady Seraphina and did not wish to be strong-armed into marriage to a woman he did not care for by his aunt.

Increasingly aware of the narrowing circle of his own choices, Adam was willing to take a risk. It would undoubtedly help *him*, and if it assisted Lady Emilia in the process then it would be all the better.

"If you will excuse me, aunt," he said suddenly, making up his mind. "I am going to get some air."

CHAPTER THIRTEEN

His aunt frowned at him in response, but he did not give her time to reply. He placed his wine glass behind him and walked as discreetly as he could around the dancefloor and towards the doorway.

He kept his gaze downcast until he reached it, glancing behind him to find that most of the guests were either involved in the dance or watching it. Lionel stood in the centre of the current set, opposite Miss Fairfax. His cousin's wide smile and relaxed movements sent a pang of regret through Adam's body, but as his gaze fell on Seraphina, he felt all the more determined to follow through with his plan.

He compressed the handle of the door and moved outside.

The bitter cold hit him full in the face as he closed the door behind him. The snow was falling but in much smaller flakes than it had earlier that day and there were patches of ice over the terrace.

He looked along the narrow walkway to see a figure ahead of him, her breath billowing out above her as she looked out into the night.

The clouds obscured the stars but lowered a blanket of snow across the country, making everything look ghostly and magical at once.

Adam approached her, feeling his heart beating so wildly he could barely draw in a full breath. His chest was tight, his fists clenched. He felt as though he were standing on the edge of an abyss and that the only guiding light to reach the other side was standing before him.

For the first time since Anastasia's death, he felt a desire for companionship. His interactions with Emilia had been some of the easiest in his life, and the way her music sang to his soul could not be anything but a sign he was ready to move forward.

She was no longer simply a woman dogged by scandal, forced to live a life of her parents' choosing. Adam was no longer simply a widower mourning his wife—he believed they could help one another, and in time, a true connection could form between them that might be the greatest he had ever known.

"Lady Emilia," he said softly, watching in wonder as she turned to him.

Emilia had been standing on the terrace for too long, and her fingers were numb already, but she was reluctant to return inside. She knew what awaited her in that ballroom, and it was nothing in the world that she wanted.

Her mind had been playing tricks on her, focusing on a dark future where she watched as Lord Bellebrook announced his engagement to Lady Seraphina. Emilia stood idly in the shadows, married and miserable, with the duke by her side.

Then she heard her name uttered behind her from the one voice she had never expected to hear.

Stunned, she turned to find herself alone with the earl. She felt her heart skip a beat in her chest, her eyes widening in amazement.

"Lord Bellebrook," she managed with a smile. She could think of nothing else to say.

"Lady Emilia, I hope you will not think we too forward, but I felt compelled to follow you tonight."

Emilia could not breathe, her fingers pulling at the side of her gown, the impossible promise in his words seemingly beyond her wildest imaginings.

"I shall come directly to the point, Lady Emilia. I fear we do not have much time until we are both frozen statues of ice after all." He huffed a laugh but took a step forward, his gaze earnest. "You and I... I believe we have a connection. It may be fleeting at present, but I wish to be honest with you. Lord knows the world in which we live is designed to deceive, and I wanted to ask you, truthfully, do you wish to marry the Duke of Elderbridge?"

Emilia stared at him, amazed by his direct question and alarmed by her own response to it.

Never in my worst nightmares.

"No," she said softly. She could see his breath mixing with hers only feet from her, his eyes twinkling in the darkness. "No, but my parents wish it for me."

"My aunt wishes for me to marry Lady Seraphina."

Emilia nodded. "It would be a suitable match."

"It is not. Not to me." He paused, taking a smaller step forward again. "Lady Emilia, I have been captivated by you these last few days. Since the first moment I heard you play, I have felt something within me that is linked to you in ways I cannot explain. I know we do not know one another well, but we are both in difficult positions neither one of us would choose. I am not merely asking this for the sake of your life but for my own, too."

Emilia's breath shuddered before her, her lungs screaming, her heart pattering a staccato rhythm so violent she thought it might burst out of her chest altogether.

"You might think me mad, but I believe we can help one another and forge a new future together. I am asking, my Lady, if you would do me the honour of agreeing to marry me."

***

The night sky felt endless, the countryside about them unravelling before them like a spool of ribbon into the darkness.

Emilia would never have dreamed that Lord Bellebrook would have come out here to say such a thing. What was more alarming was the all-encompassing relief and joy that his proposal brought for her.

I will be free of the duke, she thought happily, *and I will have a good man of good reputation to call my own. How have I been so lucky?*

She did not speak for a moment, watching his handsome face contort into worry and concern.

"I know that—"

"Yes, my Lord. I accept."

There was a frozen moment of stillness in the dark between them. An owl hooted, and the strains of the music from the ballroom looped and spiralled in the air.

A smile bloomed over Adam's face, so wide that Emilia was enraptured by it, and he let out a long breath as though all of his prayers had been answered at once.

"You are sure?"

She answered his smile with one of her own. "I am," she nodded urgently. "You are right, we have not known one another long, but I admire you for your honesty and candour, my Lord. I would count myself very lucky to be able to call you my husband."

He took another step forward, the cold world around them seemed quite warm in that moment. As though they were cocooned in their own private wonderland.

"But we should be careful," Emilia continued. "An abrupt announcement would arouse suspicion, particularly in a setting such as this."

Adam looked back at the lighted windows of the ballroom, a frown marring his handsome features and he nodded.

"Yes, you are right. What would you propose?"

"We have been seen together already, of course, but I would say that we could make it known over the next few days that we are closer than we had been. Our relationship could unfold more naturally to those present, and the conclusion will not be so shocking."

Adam nodded. "I suppose I could ask for your hand after Christmas."

Emilia felt alive with excitement, and she could see the same expression on Adam's face.

"I suppose it would not seem honest to many, but I have no qualms in deceiving the gossipmongers for a little time; they have done me no favours over the years, after all."

Adam grinned now, his wide smile invoking the same calmness and contentment that Emilia had experienced before.

"No, indeed. I would not wish to deceive my aunt, but I have been becoming increasingly concerned that *any* attention to Lady Seraphina will lead me down a dangerous path. Perhaps we can agree that we will not allow ourselves to be cornered by... undesirable members of the party."

That surprised a laugh from her, and Emilia covered her mouth, concerned about being overheard as Adam gave her an answering smile.

"Yes, that might suit me very well."

"The duke is a persistent man," Adam stated, his voice lowering, his expression darkening.

"Indeed. And the marquess' daughter speaks enough words for the whole party put together."

Adam snorted, straightening as he collected himself, his eyes full of mischief. There was palpable excitement and happiness between them now, and Emilia felt as though she could float away into the night and never have another care in the world.

"Thank you for your honesty, my Lord," she said sincerely. "I appreciate it more than I can say. And I have truly enjoyed your company. I can only hope we will have a good partnership."

"I hope the same. More than you know." He glanced behind him furtively. "We should return before we are missed. You should precede me, and I will walk around the other side. I would not wish anyone to see us together unchaperoned; I would hate for it to cast even a shadow upon your reputation."

Emilia smiled and nodded. "I suppose I shall see you inside, then."

"Indeed, you shall. Might I request the honour of the next dance? I shall endeavour not to tread upon the toes of my intended."

Emilia's fluttering laugh came easily, and she could not help but smile as she made her way to the door.

"I should be very pleased to dance with you, Lord Bellebrook."

"Then I shall look forward to it, Lady Emilia."

CHAPTER FOURTEEN

It took a moment for Emilia to remember where she was the following morning.

There was the chirp of birdsong outside her window and a bright light all around her room. She lay silently in her bed, listening to the world waking up around her, wondering why she felt so content.

Then the conversation with Adam came back to her. *Lord Bellebrook,* she reminded herself with a small smile.

She was still stunned that it had taken place at all. It was astounding to her that this unassuming and kind man liked her enough not only to tell her he was captivated by her, but to offer her his hand in marriage.

She pushed back the blankets on her bed and stood, walking across the cold wooden floors to the windows. It was the same view she had admired only days before, but somehow the world looked better and brighter this morning.

I am finally free of the duke, she thought in ecstasy.

The feeling was wonderful but bittersweet. Emilia knew, that no matter how much she liked and admired Lord Bellebrook, this was a marriage of convenience. He would no longer have to be pushed toward Lady Seraphina Cheswick—a fact that gave her vicious pleasure—and she would not have to marry the Duke of Elderbridge.

She sighed, looking out into the wintry day before her and feeling festive with the joys of the season. Thinking to the night before reminded her that she needed to speak with Charlotte. It might be unwise to share what had taken place with the earl just yet, but it was not only that which she wished to speak with her friend about.

She had noticed that Charlotte and Lord Spencer had maximised their opportunities on the dance floor, hardly parting for the remainder of the evening, and had never seen Charlotte laugh so heartily. *That* seemed like a love match if ever she had seen one.

She thought of Adam's kind face, his twinkling eyes, and his mischievous smile. Perhaps she could hold some hope that, given time, he might feel that way toward her. Until then, she had to go downstairs and face a household of guests who she would be lying to for the majority of the next few days—including her own parents.

She thought of Charlotte, guilt weighing heavily within her at keeping the truth from her, but she was unsure if her friend would be able to keep it to herself around Lord Spencer. If it were to get out she would have far more trouble on her hands than she needed.

A gentle knock on the door announced the arrival of her maid and she began to get ready for the day, a spring in her step and excitement in her heart for the first time in weeks.

***

Adam sat beside Lionel in a daze. He had some eggs and buttered toast on his plate, but nothing felt real.

What on earth have I done?

There was no denying that the moment Emilia had agreed to his proposal, he had felt elated. That feeling still lingered, but it was mixed with the guilt that swirled about his mind every day.

He swallowed, picking up his cup of coffee and trying to tune into the conversations around him. Lord and Lady Sternwood were discussing hanging ornaments as their Christmas activity of the day. Along the table, the Pinkertons remarked upon the excellent breakfast that had been laid out for them. Adam felt distanced from it all—the world around him was like a dream world he had accidentally stumbled into.

So much of the last three years had been shrouded in sadness and melancholy that he felt like an entirely different person this morning. Anastasia was never far from his thoughts, but Emilia's presence had somehow combined with hers to lighten his mood and make her memory sharper and keener—it was almost as though Emilia had made it less painful to remember her.

How strange life can be at times.

Feeling eyes upon him, he looked up into Frederick's assessing gaze. Having been caught watching him, Frederick schooled his expression into a more neutral one, but Adam had seen the calculating assessment in his face.

What could have angered him already? It is not even ten o'clock.

With a jolt, he wondered if Frederick had dipped too deep again the night before. He had been so distracted by his own plans; he had not kept an eye on him. Adam glanced at Lord Sternwood, and sure enough, the man's gaze returned to Frederick time and again, trying to catch his eye.

This was a familiar dance.

Frederick would always win hands of cards to start with. Successful gamblers, if one could describe them as such, knew to quit while they were ahead. Frederick had never had that ability and clearly his luck had run out. Adam recognised the signs immediately, and he was mortified on behalf of his cousin that Lord Sternwood might be out of pocket.

Adam was convinced Frederick would ask him for a loan again. He had done it before, and Adam had been fool enough to agree. But not this time. He would not be party to a repayment of a debt for his future father-in-law. The idea that he would soon be part of Lord Sternwood's family was alarming in its way, but at least he finally knew the direction of his future.

Adam could not deny that he would have preferred a love match, but considering how far he had come in only a matter of days, he was hopeful. His heart was light and full again, and the pain he carried was lessening day by day. Perhaps he could be content with that.

Then the door of the room opened, and the object of his thoughts entered in a waft of cinnamon-laced air.

Adam stared.

Emilia looked exquisite. Her hair was up in a complicated twist at the back of her head, and small yellow flowers were placed within the plaits to match the gold of her dress. She looked like an angel, and it was not until she walked further into the room and Lionel nudged Adam's elbow that he realised he was staring.

As Emilia walked to her seat, it occurred to him that the future he had craved might still be within his reach. What was to stop them from deepening their connection?

As Emilia reached her chair, Adam's jaw clenched as the duke stood up and pulled it out for her. Adam could instantly see the tensing of Emilia's body in the man's presence and wanted to leap across the table and push him out of the way.

He sipped his coffee, keeping his eye on them as discreetly as possible.

Emilia sat down, smoothing her skirts over her knees as she tried to pluck up the courage to look at Adam. Elderbridge poured her a cup of tea she had not asked for, she would much have preferred coffee this morning. He handed her several slices of toast with his fingers and placed them on her plate.

Does the man think he can dictate what I eat as well as who I marry?

She finally managed to glance at Adam, her heart leaping in her chest at the furious expression on his face as he surveyed the duke.

We are engaged to be married.

The knowledge was jarring and strange as she watched Seraphina take her seat beside Adam. His attention was diverted briefly, and Emilia tried not to stare at them as Seraphina bid him good morning. She was very unlike Emilia in looks, all sparkling diamonds and blonde hair.

But Adam said he did not want her, she reminded herself. *Just as I do not want—*

"And how are you this morning, Lady Emilia?" the duke asked her with his mouth full of egg. There was a drop of yolk on his chin that he had missed and it was adhering to the faint stubble that protruded from his skin.

"Very well, your Grace, and you?"

"Oh, I always sleep very well. I have an excellent constitution and all that," he laughed heartily, and Emilia almost rolled her eyes when her father joined in with the joke.

"That is good, your Grace," she replied weakly.

"It is. When one has so much to attend to in the day, it is unarguably improved with a good night's rest. My bedroom at the estate looks out on the lake, which is teaming with fish. You must come to visit one of these days with your family."

Emilia glanced at her mother, who was positively bouncing in her seat at the invitation. She felt ill at the thought and had to remind herself again that if her agreement with Lord Bellebrook came to fruition, she would never have to entertain the duke's whims.

Lord Fairfax began speaking to her father about the arrival of his new gelding and the duke jumped on the chance to talk of the 'prize stallions' at his estate. Emilia listened with half an ear, conscious that she was not being particularly lively or interesting this morning.

Adam appeared to be listening to Seraphina, and Emilia glanced at him only to catch his eye. He had the same mischievous expression from the night before, and he hid a smile as Seraphina's conversation became plainer. Apparently, the design of the teacups was *exactly* like the ones she had at home. It appeared she had been speaking on the topic for many minutes.

With a rush of acute joy, Emilia hid a smile behind her teacup, knowing that they were sharing in a joke that only they were privy to. It was surprising to her how comfortable she already felt in his presence, and as she finished her tea and swallowed the last of her food, even the duke's arrogant chatter could not reduce her good mood.

As the breakfast was cleared away and the guests rose to their feet, Adam put a hand on Lionel's arm and stopped him from leaving the room.

"I might walk around the grounds for a little time," he said loudly.

"Oh!" Miss Fairfax exclaimed, taking the bate immediately with a smile. "Emilia, I would adore a stroll around the gardens. Might we come with you, my Lord?"

Her expression was all innocence, but Adam wasn't fooled. "It would be an honour, Miss Fairfax."

"Oh," Emilia said, looking a little flustered. "Yes, that would be excellent."

After they had donned their cloaks and gathered their gloves and hats, they met in the main entrance hall of the house.

Adam offered Emilia his arm, and a shudder of awareness ran through him as she took it. The simple gesture felt far more significant than it should, given the secret nature of their agreement and that cocoon that had seemed to envelop them the night before returned.

Adam realised he would have been content to spend all day with her just walking around the house or the gardens, enjoying her company.

They made their way outside into the thick snow. The paths had been cleared earlier that day, but their feet still crunched over the icy ground as they walked around the corner of the house.

Charlotte held Lord Spencer's arm in easy silence as they walked behind their friends. Both had acknowledged their suspicions of what was growing between Emilia and the Earl of Bellebrook, and Charlotte was incredibly happy for Emilia.

If anyone deserved to meet a good man and be joyful, it was her. Charlotte's thoughts turned to her own good fortune and the man walking beside her. Lionel was quiet and contemplative that morning, but when she turned to him, his eyes were alert and bright.

"It is strange, is it not, how mistletoe finds a way to survive during the coldest month of the year," Lionel said casually as they passed beneath a towering tree with bunches of mistletoe growing haphazardly through the branches.

"Do you think so, my Lord?" Miss Fairfax asked all polite interest.

"Indeed I do. It would appear that winter is the most barren season," he said, watching Adam in front of him, as Miss Fairfax followed his gaze, "and yet, with the right conditions and a nurturing branch to live upon, it flourishes."

Miss Fairfax had a smile on her face now, her eyes dancing with amusement. "You are right, of course," she said contentedly. "Much can come from barren earth after all."

"I couldn't agree more," Lionel replied, tightening his arm in hers and feeling the pressure return as they continued walking. After a short time, they passed a particularly large patch of lawn, and an idea occurred to him: "I say!"

Adam turned to him, releasing Emilia who stood beside him looking at Lionel expectantly. He was struck by just what a handsome couple they made.

"Do you know it's been an age since I last crafted a snow figure?"

Adam looked down at Emilia and any reticence he might have had faded away at the excitement in her eyes.

"Oh, I haven't made a snowman since I was a child!"

"A competition," Miss Fairfax declared, dashing into the centre of the garden, careless for the virgin picture she had destroyed with her footprints. "Lord Spencer, you are hereby charged with crafting the base."

Lionel laughed that infectious booming laugh of his and dutifully followed her instructions, beginning to push a small snowball around the garden as Charlotte gathered sticks and began preparing the head.

Adam turned to Emilia, who had already begun working alongside Charlotte. "It seems we are a pair once more," she said with a lightness that drew him in, and he found himself following her without a second thought.

"So it would appear," he replied softly, as Emilia grinned back at him and set to work on their creation.

The base began to take shape quickly, but it was not long before she struggled to push it along by herself, collapsing into fits of giggles.

Adam stepped up manfully to assist her and they began to push it together but it wasn't until his gloved hand covered hers that the chill of the cold faded away entirely and Adam became altogether too warm.

For a moment, the weight of their arrangement settled heavily between them. Emilia's cheeks flushed prettily, her hazel-green eyes lifting to meet his. Neither moved to pull away, his hand remaining over hers, the world around them fading as his heart thundered in his chest.

But their brief seconds of connection were swiftly shattered by a well-aimed snowball. Emilia shrieked with mock defiance as Charlotte ran away excitedly, Emilia pursuing her as though they were children, throwing handfuls of snow as they both doubled over in fits of giggles. Adam was laughing himself until a snowball hit him squarely in the face from Lionel, and the fight was on.

His cousin sprinted behind a tree, but Adam was too quick for him and landed one in the small of his back before he could hide from him completely. Emilia's genuine, high-pitched laughter was a joy to hear. She was uninhibited, flushed from the cold, and happier than he had ever seen her.

I want to make her smile like that for the rest of my life.

The thought was crystal clear, and as the game continued—the two women teaming up to pelt the men with snow—Adam's cheeks ached with the mad joy of it all.

From the house behind them at an upper window, a face looked down on the little party with a grim expression.

Watching Adam in the garden made a bitter taste form in Frederick's mouth. He noted how his cousin rarely looked away from Emilia, his features softening when he smiled at her. It was an expression Frederick had seldom seen from him, even when he had been with Anastasia. There was something pure and wholesome about the connection between the two of them, and he knew he would be hard-pressed to rip it apart.

He would, though. He had no choice.

Adam would lose any interest in her and return to his lonely dark house for the rest of his days, and Frederick would finally receive what was owed to him. He already owed fifteen pounds to Lord Sternwood on top of all the other bets he had made. But perhaps the man could be persuaded to forget the debt when the news of his daughter's marriage to the duke was announced.

CHAPTER FIFTEEN

As the group went back inside, rosy-cheeked and in high spirits, they joined the other guests for hot chocolate and biscuits.

As Emilia stepped back into the drawing room beside Adam her heart raced, a flutter of unease tightening her chest. It felt surreal to be standing beside him, to be *engaged* to him when no one around them knew the truth.

She glanced at him as he surveyed the room, his eyes reminding her of the shallow shores at the beach when she was a child, the clear blue water calling to her against the white sands of the Cornish coast.

In the gardens, she had begun to see the playful side of the earl, and it warmed her heart. When they had first met, he had been reserved and quiet, unhappy even. She had not been certain he had wished to be a member of their company or to be part of the house party at all. Yet now, he seemed to be lighter in himself and some of the tension had left his face.

As though sensing her look, Adam turned, and Emilia's heart thudded wildly in her chest as his eyes softened offering her a shallow bow before walking across the room to speak with his aunt.

He was so *handsome* that was what she could not understand. *Why would someone such as he look at me, a woman who society has shunned for years?*

"You are looking melancholy, and I cannot fathom why. You have every reason to be cheerful," Charlotte said, coming up behind her.

Emilia was about to reply with a denial when she was jolted to the side by someone walking swiftly through the room. Righting herself, she turned back to see Frederick Bentley. He had stopped, his jaw working as he bowed to her, his hand on his chest in apology. Emilia held back a gasp at the look of quiet fury on his face, but it was wiped clean as soon as their eyes met.

"My apologies, my Lady, I was not looking where I was walking."

"No matter, Mr Bentley," Emilia replied, attempting a smile, "No harm has been done."

Frederick gave her a tight nod and continued on his way towards Adam and Augusta.

Emilia felt a shiver run through her that she could not name and glanced at Charlotte.

"I wondered if my aversion to that man was simply my own," Charlotte said darkly. "There is something very odd about him. Do you know, during the ball, he stood by the wall and simply stared at you for several minutes together? I thought it might simply be that I'd misinterpreted the direction in which he was looking, but he has done it several times since. I considered whether he might be thinking of making an advance."

Emilia shook her head. "How strange. That is the first time we have spoken; he has certainly not sought me out at any point."

"Perhaps he is shy," Charlotte mused. The two women exchanged a glance, and Charlotte's lips pursed together. "No, you are right. I do not believe that either."

"He looked at me like he hated me. Perhaps he has heard of the scandal and does not approve of—" She stopped abruptly, realising she had been about to reveal Adam's attachment to her.

"Approve of what?" Charlotte asked indignantly, always quick to come to her defence. "You have done nothing, broken no laws and slighted nobody. Anyone who is still harping on about such things is not welcome in my company I can promise you that."

Emilia leaned into her friend gratefully. "You are too good to me."

"I know," Charlotte said with a put-upon sigh, making Emilia laugh, "I do not know why I put up with you at all. You are so tiresome."

Emilia chuckled, and Charlotte grinned at her mischievously.

"Speaking of attachments," Emilia said carefully. "You and Lord Spencer do seem to be getting along well together. I rather thought you believed him to be very stupid."

Charlotte eyed her friend, unsure whether to express the depths of her feelings for Lord Spencer. She had never met anyone she liked so much, who was so well connected and so generous with his spirit and feeling.

Charlotte was not a romantic. She knew full well that connections in society, particularly at this time of year, could easily be misinterpreted. Lord Spencer had shown her much attention over the last few days, but it was only that—attention. She had never been someone who fell all over herself for the sake of a handsome man, but there was a part of her that wanted to grasp her friend's hand and tell her she was enraptured.

He was so genial and polite, never overstepping his bounds. Charlotte was aware that Emilia and Lord Bellebrook had grown close, but Adam was rather too serious for Charlotte's tastes. Lord Spencer was all levity, smiles, and excitement. Charlotte had been startled by how much she liked him and their time in the gardens had been the happiest she had ever spent with anyone.

"I am not certain," she said cautiously, "to what you are referring."

Emilia, with that intuitive manner she sometimes possessed, seemed to read her perfectly, however, and Charlotte's anxiety was quelled as her friend took her hand.

"You and I have spoken at length of the connections we can expect in life. I would never presume to make one for you."

"I know," Charlotte said, watching Lord Spencer across the room speaking with Emilia's father. "I had no significant interest for the whole of last season. I was beginning to believe it was hopeless. I am still bemused as to how a man such as he can be unattached. I cannot fathom it."

"Perhaps he was waiting for you," Emilia said wistfully. "Stranger things have happened, and you are the loveliest creature imaginable."

"Do be quiet, you will make me blush," Charlotte protested, but her friend's words had given her comfort. She knew her parents were desperate for her to make a good match, and she was determined not to allow their worries to affect her.

Lady Sternwood clapped her hands for attention at the head of the room and smiled about at the group.

"We will be decorating the Christmas tree in the entrance hall and dressing the corridors this morning. When you have all finished your drinks, please make your way through, and I will show you the beautiful creations that are waiting to be hung."

"Do you think we will be hanging them terribly high?" Lady Seraphina said as she passed Adam and his aunt. "I simply cannot abide heights; I am so frightfully afraid of heights."

"Not to worry, my dear," said his aunt as she bustled forward. "There will be plenty of strapping young men to help us," she exclaimed, taking Seraphina's arm and giving Adam a long stare before leaving the room.

"I love my mother," Lionel said softly, "but she is trying even *my* patience with this. Does she not see you have other things on your mind?"

Adam's head snapped around to look at his cousin, but Lionel just gave him a playful wink and followed his mother out of the room. As he did so, Adam's eye was drawn to Emilia, who was standing with Miss Fairfax on the other side of the carpeted entryway before him.

She still looked flushed from their impromptu snowball fight, and her eyes were sparkling as she looked about the room.

A feeling of unease crept over him as he considered the offer he had made the night before. He did not regret it—far from it—but it was still an adjustment to realise that this woman was his betrothed. He rubbed his hands together, fiddling with his shirt sleeves, trying to pull himself back to the present. He could hear the lively chatter of those who had already moved into the hallway and the clink of decorations as they were removed from their boxes. Adam nabbed another biscuit to calm his nerves and attempted to revel in the unexpected joys of the season.

I have never appreciated Christmas so much as I have in Lady Emilia's company.

***

As they made their way into the entrance hall, Emilia looked up at the beautiful garlands hanging from the doorway and the leafless tree branches her mother had brought in from outside to be adorned with decorations.

Everything looked glorious—the large Christmas tree at the base of the stairs was truly magnificent and sent a surge of excitement through her. With the snow on the ground outside and the snowball fight, not to mention her blossoming friendship with Lord Bellebrook, she felt happy and excited for the holidays.

Her mother handed her a box of crystal-cut ornaments that sparkled in the light, and Emilia placed the box on a chair as Lady Pinkerton and her husband approached and collected some of them.

"These are quite exquisite!" Lady Pinkerton exclaimed, holding one of them up to the light as rainbows danced across the floor in its wake. "I am so overwhelmed by all your mother has done. Does it not look beautiful in the house?"

"It truly does," her husband agreed, looking down at his wife adoringly. Emilia watched the gentle exchange between the two of them and felt a pang of loss that the love between them might never be her fate.

"Lady Emilia, allow me to help you."

Emilia turned to look up at the duke who towered above her, smirking down at her in that infuriating way of his.

On second thoughts, I do not need love. She thought desperately. *I just need to be away from this man for the rest of my life.*

She nodded to the duke, holding out the box to him. Behind him she noticed Adam entering the entrance hall, his eyes on them, his jaw tightening with obvious displeasure. Emilia wondered if he might come over to save her, but he was pulled aside by his cousin Frederick. She was thus left to endure the duke's simpering conversation and idle prattle.

"I was most surprised by your behaviour in the gardens, Lady Emilia," the duke said. Emilia glanced up at him in alarm. His expression was reserved and carefully polite, but his eyes were hard. "I had not seen that side of you. I must say I was shocked that you would behave in such an unladylike manner."

Emilia's hands shook as she took another ornament from the box, but this time, it was not with nerves but rage. Apparently, the duke did not want his future wife to display any kind of excitement, happiness, or joy, even at Christmas. It was a damning testimony to any type of life she might have had in his company, and she was even more grateful to the Earl of Bellebrook for saving her from it.

As Adam's eyes lingered on Emilia's back, a fresh wave of jealousy surged through him, but this time, it was far more violent in its intensity. He frowned at Frederick who placed an impertinent hand on his sleeve. The man seemed agitated and there was sweat adhering to his brow despite the high ceilings of the entrance hall and a rather chill breeze through the front door.

"Is all well?" Adam asked, feigning ignorance, but he knew exactly what Frederick would ask of him.

"Of course, of course," his cousin said meekly. "I merely wished to ensure *you* were well."

Adam was not too proud to admit that he was surprised the man even noticed other people, but he nodded all the same. His eyes flicked to Emilia and the duke, fingers flexing to prevent him from striding across to them and shoving the man to the floor.

"Yes, I am quite well. Why would I not be?"

"Simply that I know how much you loved spending Christmas with Anastasia."

Adam froze, guilt slicing through him. He knew he should ignore his cousin's words, but his conscience weighed heavily upon him. He felt an undeniable sense of remorse that he could neither escape nor suppress.

Adam's heart clenched at the thought of Anastasia and how much she would have loved this house party.

What would she think of me? He thought sadly. *Running about in the gardens with another woman playing with snowballs when she is gone forever and can never enjoy such things again.*

Adam's mood darkened considerably, and he glanced at his cousin, who had his eyebrows raised in query.

"I am sorry, I did not mean to—"

"No matter," Adam replied curtly. "I must help my aunt."

He walked across the room, his head held high, as he reached Augusta. With the large Christmas tree obscuring her, Adam had not realised his aunt stood beside Lady Seraphina. To his dismay, Augusta departed almost instantly, and Adam was left awkwardly standing beside her as she gave him a shy smile.

Adam glanced to his right, noting that the duke was still very close to Emilia, who was pale and taut beside him. Frederick's words were still ringing in his ears, but there was no denying he hated seeing Emilia with another man.

He knew all too well that their arrangement was a convenience, but Adam felt a pulse of anger that dimmed his guilt.

The duke does not have a claim to her. I do. And I cannot even warn him off because nobody knows the truth.

CHAPTER SIXTEEN

Emilia stood in her bedroom and pulled on her coat as the party prepared to walk to the local village.

The morning air was brisk and cold, and the house was bustling with movement as the guests prepared to depart. She rubbed her hands together against the cold, recalling the comforting warmth of Lord Bellebrook's arm wrapped around hers the day before.

Everything still seemed surreal, but her strange sense of happiness in his presence was also clouded by guilt. Emilia knew what her parents were expecting and how they valued the duke's connection. They were still adamant that he was the best possible choice for her despite so many reasons why their match did not make sense in Emilia's eyes.

She looked beyond to the beautiful world outside and walked to the fireplace, touching the holly leaves that were scattered across its surface.

When her world had fallen apart after her discussion with Lord Blackmoor, she had been numb to many emotions. It was strange to remember how much she had ignored from the past few years. It had not just been the bad feelings but also the good ones. Any emotion at all had been suppressed in her mind, and in the last few days, she was beginning to feel them come alive again.

Her heart felt full, and the Christmas season suddenly seemed joyous. She looked at the snow and the winter wonderland outside her window, and it seemed more beautiful than it ever had before. Emilia was excited for Christmas day. It would herald the penultimate moment before Adam would speak to her father, and a new future would be sealed for her.

Sophia, Penelope, and Caroline would be pleased, she thought, with a small smile. *They will not have to endure the insult of me becoming their mother, after all.*

Emilia jolted in surprise, pulled from her thoughts, as she heard her mother's voice drifting up the stairs and realised that she had lingered at her window for too long and would need to go down to meet the other guests.

Adam was waiting alongside Lionel when Emilia emerged at the head of the staircase. Her gaze was uncertain as she looked about the company, her hand held tightly to the bannister. Adam felt a bolt of happiness when her eyes alighted on his, and she appeared to relax. He came forward, waiting for her at the base of the stairs. Lady Sternwood was not far away from him, and he noticed her watching them as Emilia descended. Adam kept his face carefully blank but was aware that if they were to make the company believe their relationship had blossomed over the coming days, he would have to make it clear to her parents that he had an interest in their daughter.

Emilia reached the bottom step, taking a deep breath as she did so. Adam smiled and nodded to her in greeting.

"Good morning, Lady Emilia," he said quietly, aware of the smile tugging at his lips. Adam knew they were not being entirely honest with those around them, but he was finding that he enjoyed having a secret that only he and Emilia were privy to.

"Good morning, Lord Bellebrook," she said happily, looking about her. All the baskets they had prepared were assembled on a table beside the front door, and she ran her eyes over them appreciatively. "Have you managed to locate your creation amidst the throng?"

"I have. It is a pitiful sight. I believe I shall tuck it away to spare anyone the misfortune of displaying it in their home."

She laughed in a light, pleasing way and stepped down the last step as the rest of the group came together. Adam was conscious of eyes on him and looked up at Lady Sternwood, only to find Frederick watching him. The man had such a look of loathing on his face that it quite chilled Adam's blood.

Adam frowned at him, and the look evaporated.

Hurriedly, Adam offered Emilia his arm as the duke entered the room. The man was flanked by his daughters, the youngest of whom was receiving a dressing down for some slight or another. The duke thankfully fell into step beside Sophia Easton, and the fact that Adam was escorting Emilia did not seem to register in his attention.

Emilia took Adam's arm, and they made their way into the village.

Despite the heavy snowfall, carriages and wagons still had to travel into the little village of Tinsdale, and labourers must have spent many hours clearing the paths.

The little gaggle of party members all walked out onto the lane, relieved to see that deep grooves existed through the snow, creating a makeshift path. Much of the main road into the village had been cleared. Unlike outside the chapel, where the snow had been growing so thick it was almost impassable, it was much easier to navigate here.

A river ran alongside the road, its babbling path over the rocks, not having allowed the water to freeze. It flowed happily down the little hill and under a bridge to their left, snow covering the banks. Adam listened to the sound, likening it to the tinkle of notes on a piano.

"How are you this morning?" he asked Emilia. They had separated now that the path was firmer, and Adam was conscious that he could not hold her arm all the way to the village without eyebrows being raised.

Nevertheless, he still wanted to and felt her absence acutely. Lionel and Miss Fairfax walked ahead of them, chattering merrily, and Adam was eager to use the time to get to know Emilia on their short walk to the village.

She did not say anything for so long he wondered whether she had heard him.

"Is all well?" he asked softly. "You are not having second thoughts?"

She glanced at him then. "No, my Lord, nothing like that. I suppose I was wondering how honest to be with you."

Adam's heart warmed at the uncertainty in her voice. "I would never wish you to feel you could not be honest with me, Lady Emilia. Even if it is a difficult thing to confess, I would know your thoughts."

"I suppose I am not sure how I feel," she said a little ruefully. "I am lighter in myself. I find that Christmas has more joy to it than it has done for many years. It is odd, but I feel I have known you for longer than I have. Does that seem strange?"

Adam clenched his fists inside his gloves, the sting of the cold grounding him somehow.

"No. I do not think it is odd. It is how I feel also."

"Truly?" she asked, a note of awe in her voice.

"Most assuredly. I wish to know you better."

"You may ask me anything."

"Anything?" he asked with a smile. "What a notion."

She laughed. "Within reason. There may be some things I will not disclose."

"Such as?"

"Oh, I do not know. Perhaps that when I think nobody is paying attention, I have been known to dip a mince pie into my tea."

Adam barked a laugh so loud that Lionel and Miss Fairfax turned around, and he quickly schooled his features.

"I am appalled," he said playfully. "I suppose I should confess then that I have hated, and will always hate, plum pudding and mince pies for long as I live."

Emilia stopped in her tracks, forcing the Pinkertons to navigate around them, and Adam was very close to a belly laugh at her expression.

Realising that she was drawing attention, Emilia continued with a deep frown that shouldn't have been so endearing.

"You do not *like* plum pudding. Even if it is covered with brandy?"

"I like brandy. Does that count?"

"It does not. Tell me you enjoy fruitcake."

"Cannot stand the stuff."

Emilia gasped in shock, and Adam chuckled, listening to the crunch of the snow beneath their feet and the chatter of the others as they neared the village.

"I simply do not know if I could marry a man who dislikes fruit cake," she said, his voice very quiet.

"Whyever not? I would think it would be a reason to do so."

"Why?" she asked, glancing at him.

"Well, you could eat it all for yourself, and I would never touch a crumb."

Emilia brightened, her hazel eyes dancing as she grinned.

"That is an excellent point, Lord Bellebrook. Perhaps I shall allow it after all."

"I am very pleased to hear it," he said, looking up at the branches of the trees above them and the beautiful day that was forming above their heads.

As they reached the village, Emilia was struck by the look of some of the houses they were approaching. The area where they were distributing the baskets was rather more ramshackle than the main street, and an urchin boy watched them suspiciously from the top of some steps to their left.

Many of the houses had tiny windows that were banked with snow, and the general feel of the place was rundown and melancholy.

Emilia was glad they had come, but she was also reminded of her own intense privilege in a world where people struggled to put food on the table.

She looked down at the baskets brimming with food and festive cheer and realised that her mother had bought all of it as a frivolity. It might give these people a happier season, but this was a luxury many could not afford.

She would go back to her manor with its endless fires and food and likely forget this world as soon as she had entered it.

"My Lady?" she looked up into Adam's face. His brow was furrowed, and he looked concerned.

"We are very lucky," she said just quietly. "I was just thinking how short a time this will all last for these people."

She wondered whether a man like Adam, who had come from the same rich background as she had, would understand her sentiment, but his expression quickly mirrored her own.

"It is a good thing we are doing," he said softly.

"So much at this time of year is about excess," she added. "These people have so little."

Adam leaned across to take the basket from her as they began to distribute them to the villagers who were beginning to gather around them. As he did so his palm briefly covered her own and she looked up into an earnest intensity that made her breath catch in her throat.

"You are right, Lady Emilia. But they have more today because of these gifts, small though they are."

She nodded, turning away from him as a woman approached carrying her infant son. She was all smiles and wished Emilia a merry Christmas, just as every single other person did. The villagers slowly began to emerge from their houses, many of them grinning widely, and Emilia watched her mother greet them all with great enthusiasm.

The streets were soon filled with people and Emilia was offered countless cups of tea to warm her, and some of the villagers even tried to give her gifts as thanks—all of which she refused.

On the other side of the square, the duke and his daughters also helped with the cause, but there was a stiffness in their movements that the other guests did not possess. It was clear this was not an activity they relished or took part in often. Some of the girls looked positively frightened of the villagers and Emilia found herself feeling sorry for them.

What a shallow life they must lead. She thought bitterly. *And they have even more than we do as a family.*

It was a morning of many emotions and feelings, but the overriding mood of those they met was unerring excitement and gratitude. It was humbling to be around so much hope, and Emilia left the village feeling as though she had been of some little use and promising that she would be back before Easter came around.

The group walked slowly back up the gradual incline to the manor. The long path was black with mud, and a mixture of snow, and the temperature seemed to have dropped since their earlier journey.

As they walked, Emilia noticed how much ice was forming beneath her feet, and as though to prove their existence, she suddenly lost her footing. A patch of thick ice took her by surprise beneath the snow and she slipped violently as she was thrown backwards.

She would have crashed painfully to the earth had not strong arms enveloped her right at the last moment, and she felt her weight suspended as Lord Bellebrook gripped her tightly to his chest.

The moment was suspended in time, his face above hers, inches away, as he balanced her weight against him. Both of them were arched back as though in the middle of a dance, an endless, sparking electricity snapping between them.

Adam blinked as Emilia pulled in a deep breath, and he slowly lifted her back to standing. A few of the group had stopped the check she was alright, and she hastily confirmed it. Glancing up she noticed Mr Frederick Bentley standing beside Lady Sophia Easton, their stares and expressions almost identical as they observed her.

"Thank you," she said breathlessly.

"Are you unharmed?" Adam's voice was far lower than it had been, and when she looked up at him, there was a heat in his gaze that she had not seen before.

"Yes, thank you, quite alright."

It was not long before they returned to the manor, and Emilia dispensed with her cloak as Lord Bellebrook and Lord Spencer walked together toward the library.

Emilia was about to join Charlotte when her mother strode across her path, her expression tight and displeased.

"A word, Emilia," she hissed, and Emilia had no choice but to follow her. She glanced behind her to see where her father had got to and saw him watching them retreat with a resigned expression.

This cannot be good. She thought miserably.

Her mother drew her into a parlour room that was rarely used. It was small and cold, and the windows faced the rear courtyard. The wallpaper was of a livid green with thrushes and cranes fluttering across it and the whole effect was rather gloomy and confused.

Her mother closed the door behind her and came to stand before her daughter, glaring at her with a calculating gaze that made Emilia want to cower into a corner.

"Explain yourself this moment," her mother insisted.

"Mama?"

"Do not play dumb with me, Emilia. What did I just witness between you and Lord Bellebrook?"

Emilia frowned. At the back of her mind, she had dared to hope that her mother would simply switch her affections seamlessly from the duke to the earl once she learned the truth. But by the expression on Lady Sternwood's face, it had been a fool's hope.

Her mother had always been a social climber, and since the scandal, she had not coped well with the doors of good society becoming closed to her. Emilia realised with depressing certainty that her mother viewed the duke as a better option for her, merely due to his title and the opportunities it might afford her.

"Mama, I merely slipped."

"He was at your side for the entirety of the morning. I have seen you speaking to one another a great deal, and do not remind me of your behaviour in the gardens yesterday. Did you want me to die of shame?"

"It was just a snowball fight, Mama."

"And you are a lady, not a child of eight."

Her mother seemed to change tack as Emilia recoiled from her and walked toward her, taking her hands and looking at her imploringly.

"Do not let the chance with the duke slip away, my dear. He is a great match. No one will be able to question your reputation if you marry him. Lord Bellebrook is a widower who has barely been seen in society since his wife's death. There have been many rumours that he will never remarry and that he was so in love with Anastasia Bentley that his heart will never be mended." She squeezed Emilia's fingers painfully. "The duke knows what he wants and has been clear with me and your father. What has Lord Bellebrook done? Nothing. You cannot trust anyone who does not make their intentions clear."

He has proposed to me, Mama. Is that clear enough?

"Yes, Mama."

"I wish to see you settled in life. I always have."

Emilia noted the use of the word 'settled,' not 'happy.' Her mother wanted to return to the exalted halls of her peers and be welcomed with open arms. The duke's status and his eldest daughters' advantageous marriages would allow her mother to circulate in the higher echelons that she craved. Emilia knew how much that would mean to both of her parents, and she wished she could be selfless enough to grant it to them.

But the idea of the duke marrying her, or even being *close* to her, revolted her. To her surprise, another thought immediately followed the other, and she found herself wondering what it might be like if Lord Bellebrook were to take her hand or perhaps brush her arm. The thought brought a warm flush to her cheeks, which she hoped her mother's sharp gaze had not noticed.

"Choose wisely, my dear. Life does not give us these chances often."

Without another word, her mother swept from the room, leaving Emilia in a tangle of confusion and uncertainty.

CHAPTER SEVENTEEN

Adam and Lionel had settled themselves before the fire in the library. The snow had begun to fall again and it was cozy and warm inside the room.

To Adam's great amusement, Lionel was still reading Keats' poetry, determined to finish it and tell Miss Fairfax his thoughts before Christmas. It appeared that simply *reading* the thing was not good enough. Lionel had already finished it twice and was trying to fathom all the hidden meanings within each poem in order to impress the lady.

Adam left his cousin to it. Lionel was always calm and quiet, and they fell into a companionable silence for many minutes until there was a knock on the door.

Both men looked up as Adam's aunt poked her head around it, seemingly relieved to see that Adam was present.

"Did you need me, Mama?" Lionel asked dutifully.

"Yes, I need you to leave the room; I require a moment of Adam's time."

Lionel knew better than to argue with his mother, but he gave Adam a look of weary acceptance as he placed his book on the table between them and left the room. It was a deliberate movement on Lionel's part—he had marked his place and would return to it—a silent message that he would not leave Adam in Augusta's clutches for long.

Adam smiled after him, keeping his own book in his hand and waiting for his aunt to get to the point of her visit.

Augusta watched Lionel leave, walking further into the room and leaving the door ajar. She came to sit opposite him, and he was reminded of the moment she had arrived in his study all those days before, asking him to attend the house party.

How lucky I am that she was able to persuade me.

Augusta fidgeted in her chair for a little while, and Adam said nothing, disinclined to begin the conversation when he was almost certain he knew what this would be about.

"All I have ever wanted for you is your happiness," Augusta said finally.

Adam's fingers tightened around his book, and he cleared his throat. "I know that."

"And you know if your happiness does not lie with Lady Seraphina, all you would have to do is to tell me?"

Adam tried not to flinch as she laid a hand on his arm.

"I have noticed a change in you of late," she continued. "I thought that you might be feeling better now that you are out of the house and away from your estate, but today proved me wrong."

She leaned forward in her chair as Adam put down his book and levelled her with a long stare.

"And what happened today?" he asked, feigning innocence.

She rolled her eyes. "It could not have been plainer that there is some connection between you and Lady Emilia. She was blushing after you caught her when she fell, I was amazed the duke did not call you out. Although I believe that man would not be able to see his own nose if it were not attached to his face."

Adam snorted. "I hope you are not implying any impropriety on my part."

"Absolutely not," she said vehemently. "I know you too well, and you are too good for that. But I was surprised. I had not expected... I am *sorry*, is what I am trying to say."

"Sorry?"

"For forcing the marquess' daughter upon you. I did not know you were growing closer to Lord and Lady Sternwood's daughter."

Adam tensed, finding that he was unable to adequately explain what was happening between them. How might things have been if he had simply been honest with Augusta and told her he was not interested in Lady Seraphina from the start?

Would I still have proposed to Emilia?

The idea was a strange one. Anastasia's face still lingered at the back of his mind, but increasingly it was being replaced with another. He did not like to think that his aunt merely saw Emilia as a means to an end. The clinical nature of *securing the estate* did not fit with his view of her at all. He did not like to think of her in those terms.

"And if I have grown closer to the lady?" he asked carefully.

"Then I would be pleased for you, of course."

"Of course?"

His aunt sighed. "I want your future to be certain—for many reasons. If you are making a new connection, that is a wonderful thing."

She leaned back in her chair again, her gaze sorrowful. "I hope you know that I would never wish to force you down a path you would prefer not to tread."

"I know that, Aunt Augusta."

"There has been a lightness in your step these last few days. If Lady Emilia is the cause, then my heart rejoices at that knowledge."

She gave him a warm smile, and Adam could not help but return it. He knew his aunt had his best interests at heart; he merely wished that he could feel more settled in his decisions. Everything he did seemed to be laced with guilt and turmoil.

When Lionel did not return immediately, Augusta settled back in her chair and they both watched the fire together, not needing to speak further, the weight of expectation lifting a little from Adam's shoulders.

The fire crackled merrily in the grate, casting shadows that spread across the shelves and toward the door. From the other side of it, visible through the crack where it remained ajar, two eyes watched the pair through the gap in the hinges as Frederick processed what he had heard.

Every passing word made the fear in his gut multiply to an unbearable degree and he knew if there was ever a time to act, it was now.

***

Later that evening the guests had gathered for a festive dinner and the atmosphere was lively as the main course of duck was served.

Charlotte and Lord Spencer had been placed opposite Emilia and Adam. They were having a lively discussion with the Pinkertons about Lord Spencer's phaeton.

"Because you see," Lady Pinkerton was saying, "I have been trying to persuade Lord Pinkerton that he is too old to purchase something so high. Everyone who uses them speaks of their dangers. Why, my nephew broke his arm falling from his," she said reproachfully.

Lord Spencer cleared his throat, reaching for his glass and glancing at her.

"Madam, I am not the right person for you to be speaking to on the subject, though it pains me to say it. Every man should have a try in a High-Perch. They are elegant things—smooth and quick. Imagine the regal way you would look about Regents Park with two glistening chestnut mares before you."

Lord Pinkerton, who was a wiry, slim man in his late fifties, chortled at Lord Spencer's words and raised his glass to him.

"I believe you have picked the wrong quarry, my dear," he said happily to his wife. "I shall make inquiries the moment we are back in London."

"When you break your back falling off the thing, I shall have no sympathy," said Lady Pinkerton irritably and stabbed at a piece of duck as she continued her supper.

Lionel smiled wickedly as Adam rolled his eyes.

"Do you have a phaeton, my Lord?" Emilia turned to Adam.

"I am of the same opinion as Lady Pinkerton—death traps the lot of them."

"Poppycock!" Lionel cried, and Emilia watched Charlotte's shoulders shudder with mirth as she tried to keep her composure.

But away from their merriment, at the other end of the table, Emilia could see the duke speaking with her father. She shifted in her seat, wondering whether he had noticed the attention Lord Bellebrook had shown her that day and what he might think of it.

"I much prefer a concert hall and a glass of port," Adam added, chewing thoughtfully on a piece of duck as Charlotte gave Emilia a meaningful look.

"Emilia and I went to see Clementi at Hanover Square in the summer," Charlotte said, "it was exquisite."

"Oh, I would give anything to be able to play like him," Emilia said. "It was a flawless performance. He was wearing blue shoes!"

Adam laughed as Miss Fairfax began to name some of the pieces they had heard at the concert to Lionel. His cousin had never had much interest in music and nodded with polite attention, but Emilia positively came alive with the topic.

She had appeared somewhat reserved since their agreement, both of them conscious that they were walking a fine line between propriety and scandal, but now she was incredibly animated.

He would have given a great deal to stand up and claim Lady Emilia right there, putting the duke off forever, but he knew it was impossible. They would have to grow their connection in a way that would be remarked upon but not overt. It was a difficult balance, and Emilia had been stiff and quiet up until this point.

Adam watched her enthusiasm with a growing sense of affection and pride. He loved hearing her speak of music—she clearly adored everything about it. He made a promise to himself that when they were married, he would take her to a concert every week.

"I lost my grandmother several years ago," Emilia explained to Lionel. "She was the one who instilled in me my love of music. It was she who took me to my first concert." Her voice was low and gentle. "She is what made me who I am today. I would not have adored the pianoforte quite so much if I had not heard her play."

"Have you thought any more of your own compositions?" Adam asked eagerly, finding himself curious as to what Emilia might create if she were to write some music herself.

Miss Fairfax was looking at him strangely, an odd little smile flitting over her face as Emilia stilled and looked across at him uncertainly.

"When one speaks of Clementi, I can only think of the great composers of our time, and it chills me to think I could think of writing anything at all."

"But you will never know," Adam said sincerely, "unless you try."

Emilia's gaze met his, and for an electric moment, he was suspended in it, the excitement infectious as her eyebrows drew together.

"Perhaps I shall try then," she said finally.

"To new beginnings."

Adam looked across at Miss Fairfax, who had raised her glass before her in a toast, staring at her friend intently.

The Pinkertons, who seemed to be two of the most enthusiastic people he had ever met, raised their glasses, too. Soon, the toast had spread around the entire table as everyone clinked their glasses, but Adam felt that something more had passed between them than a simple toast.

As he looked at Emilia's profile as she sipped her wine, he felt a sense of contentment and safety in her presence that was as surprising as it was unexpected.

The line between convenience and genuine feeling was beginning to blur, and he felt powerless to stop it. He was not even sure he wanted to.

CHAPTER EIGHTEEN

The following day, the skies were clear. Clouds that had been heavily banked with snow had moved on, and bright sunshine streamed through Adam's window.

He rose, shivering with the chill, but his chest was light, his head clear and ready to start the day.

As he looked down into the bright gardens, the snow reflecting the sunshine back against the house, he marvelled at how profoundly his life had changed in the three years since Anastasia's passing. He scratched his jaw, feeling the prickle of stubble scrape against his thumb, and glanced at the door, anxious for Villiers to come and get him dressed for the day.

When Anastasia had died, any semblance of a routine had disappeared entirely. Adam had barely eaten anything in those first few months and hadn't slept more than an hour a night.

Villiers would stand quietly behind him, razor in hand, waiting for a command that never came. Adam had been a shadow of himself, hollow-eyed and miserable.

He walked to the mirror, taking in his complexion and the shadows that still remained beneath his eyes, brushing his thumb lightly over the puffed skin. Turning his head from side to side, he examined his profile, the stubble dark against his pale jaw.

The door clicked open as Villiers entered, shoulders taut, his back straight as always. Adam watched him cross the room, floorboards creaking in his wake.

"Good morning, my Lord."

"Good morning, Villiers," Adam said, his voice tight. There was a long silence as his man began to gather his shaving equipment. "I require colour today," Adam said with determination.

Villiers hesitated, his brow knitting together as he poured hot water into the basin. "Colour, my Lord?"

"Mm. I look like a corpse."

Villiers huffed a laugh. "A little pale perhaps, my Lord."

"Did we bring anything other than my black coats? I feel as though that is all I have worn for years."

Villiers cleared his throat. "I believe that is correct, sir. But I brought the green and the blue with us, should you need them."

Adam smiled at the twinkle in his eye. He thought that this might be a day Villiers had been waiting on for some time.

"Go to it then. Try to make me look less like I have been exhumed from the earth if you possibly can."

Villiers actually laughed then as he got to work, and it occurred to Adam that he had not heard him do that for many years.

***

Lionel's gaze lingered on Adam as he sat opposite him at the breakfast table. He chewed his scrambled eggs, the buttery mixture melting against his tongue as he contemplated his friend.

"You look very smart this morning," he said as Adam glanced up at him and then down at himself in consternation. "Villiers appears to have persuaded you against black; however, did he manage it?"

"It is festive, is it not?"

"Indeed," Lionel said, his lips quirking, "and when has Adam Bentley cared for the *season* in recent years?"

Adam rolled his eyes at him as he took a large bite of his toast, and Lionel chuckled. He reached for another portion of eggs, wanting to make sure he had enough energy for the day.

They would be skating on the lake within the Sternwood estate, and Lionel was excited to spend more time with Miss Fairfax.

The guests were soon changing into thick winter coats and heading out of the manor toward the lake.

The long driveway was cleared of snow, but the cold snap overnight meant that the track had turned icy. Many of the guests were slipping and sliding all over the place and Lionel took the opportunity to offer Miss Fairfax his arm as they made their way down to the lakeside.

The lake's surface glittered with diamonds of ice, stretching unbroken to the far shore. Adam breathed in the cold air as his breath billowed around him.

Turning, his gaze fell on Emilia, who was pulling herself to her feet, the leather straps of her skates crisscrossed over her boots. She looked from the bank to the ice and back again, a small frown on her face.

He walked toward her, his skates making the short journey awkward as he tried to balance his weight against the frozen ground.

"Lady Emilia?" he asked, approaching unsteadily and letting out a small cry of alarm as his skate slid against a stone. She turned, reaching for him with a startled laugh as he launched himself against her, his muscles tensing violently as he tried to regain his balance. "My apologies," Adam added breathlessly. "I was going to enquire whether you need someone to assist you, but it appears that I am in the same position."

She chuckled. "Perhaps we can help each other, my Lord," she replied, offering him her arm. Adam linked his own through hers, the fabric of their sleeves brushing together as the warmth from her body seeped into his. "Ready my Lord?"

"Let us embark on our adventure."

They stepped down onto the lake's surface. Other members of the group were already skating in the distance, giving them certainty about the strength of the ice beneath their feet. Adam tightened his grip on Emilia's arm as he struck out against the frozen surface.

Her body pressed steadily against his side as they moved together, and the chill that had settled in his bones began to retreat. Adam's back straightened, his shoulders tightening as he relished the feeling of her arm in his, listening to the slicing crunch of their skates as they moved in long, languid strides.

The sky above them was starkly white above their head, the tiny black dots of geese in the distance the only movement to mar its perfect surface. The sounds of the other skaters slowly faded as they continued, and Adam glanced at Emilia, whose expression was soft, her eyes observing the heavily laden trees and frozen grasses around the bank.

"My mother has noticed you have been paying me some attention," Emilia said suddenly, surprising him.

Adam's stomach turned over. "What did she say?"

"That I should not let the opportunity to be with the duke pass me by," her tone was clipped, her jaw tight, and Adam felt his fingers clench into a fist as a familiar stab of jealousy spiked through his heart.

"I see," he managed, "and what did you say in return?"

"I am afraid I said very little. I know my mother well, and it is not always wise to argue."

A soft smile played over Adam's lips. "My aunt is the same. Sometimes it is best to stay silent when one knows one cannot persuade another of your point of view."

"Exactly."

"It is pleasant to be able to speak privately with you," Adam confessed.

"Just so long as we stay in plain sight, I have no wish to flirt with scandal again," her voice held a quiver, reminding him of what she had been through.

"No indeed," Adam said quickly.

Emilia's gut clenched at the sincerity in Adam's words. She felt a prickle of unease as she glanced around the lake, her eyes looking furtively from one member of the party to another. No one appeared to be watching them, but that guaranteed nothing.

On the other side of the lake, Benedict Easton wobbled onto the ice, his arms held out to the sides for balance, his gaze wild as he tried to remain upright. Caroline's peals of laughter rang out across the chilly air as his neck turned puce in the wake of her derision.

"Are you familiar with my past, my Lord?" Emilia asked. To her surprise, his arm moved at her question, placing it lightly against her lower back. The movement left their bodies much closer, and he took her hand as he steadied her. His expression was resolute, the mask of propriety falling away as he squeezed her fingers.

"I have heard some rumours about it, Lady Emilia, I will not lie to you. But I do not know the story from your own lips, and therefore, it has no weight of interest to me."

Emilia nodded. "Nothing occurred between myself and Lord Blackmoor. I am always reluctant to speak to it purely because it gives veracity to a tale if one denies it, but it is the truth."

"If it helps you, I never had any doubt."

Emilia breathed out a heavy breath at that. She had suspected he put no store by the rumours but nothing in society was ever certain.

She leaned into his body, closing her eyes for a moment at the welcome comfort it brought her.

"We were speaking of music," she continued, letting her mind go back to that day. "Lord Blackmoor, as you likely know, is married with three children now. I was speaking to him as one might to a father of an acquaintance. He had an immense passion for music, and I think was rather moved by my playing."

"I would not doubt that either."

"We were speaking for some time, and I was rather… enthused about a particular topic. He was speaking of composition. Mozart is known for his work's relative lack of errors, writing completed symphonies without any need for corrections. It is a topic I have studied myself. I have written music of my own, and it is scratched through with notes and annotations throughout. It fascinates me that Mozart saw the music on the page and simply poured a completed masterpiece onto parchment."

Emilia sighed, a chill running through her body at the memory as she swallowed around the tightness in her throat.

"I spoke to him for almost half an hour. Foolish now I come to recall it, but we were in the throes of a fascinating discussion. It was later remarked upon, and someone I had often quarrelled with in the past took the commentary and spread it about like wildfire. I was *ruined* in a single day because of a conversation about Mozart. People I had known all my life assumed I was trying to steal someone else's husband. It still boils my blood to think of it."

Adam's fingers tightened imperceptibly on her back, and Emilia sucked in a sharp breath at the feel of it. No one observing them would be able to see what he had done but the reassurance was clear.

"Thank you for sharing that with me. I hope you know that you have an ally in me, Lady Emilia. I have known you for a short time only, but I would never have suspected you were in the wrong. Society is a fickle and cruel place."

"Thank you, my Lord," Emilia said fiercely. "You have no idea how much that means to me."

They continued on, Emilia's strides more certain with the weight of the earl beside her. She felt secure and safe in his arms, and it was a feeling that was becoming more familiar by the day.

Behind Lord Bellebrook and Emilia, Charlotte had been following in their wake. She had only caught snatches of the conversation but her cheeks were flushed with happiness now. If there had been any doubt in her mind of her friend's connection to the man, it had been made a certainty now. Emilia never spoke of her scandal and rarely even discussed it with Charlotte. That she had chosen to convey her innermost secrets to Lord Bellebrook was a shocking and pleasing revelation.

"You are altogether too quick for me," came a voice from behind her, and she grinned on a half-turn to see Lord Spencer approaching her.

His answering grin was made all the more comical by his uneven gait. It appeared Lord Spencer was not altogether comfortable on the ice.

"Are you enjoying yourself, my Lord?" Charlotte asked. The gentle chatter on the lake was a faint hum in her ears, and it was liberating not to be overheard after spending so many days indoors on top of one another.

"I am now," Lord Spencer said simply, coming up beside her, his eyes twinkling.

Charlotte felt heat creep up her neck at his attentions, but she managed to glide into step with him. She watched the elegant figures of Emilia and Lord Bellebrook as they made their way to the bank to admire the view.

When she looked back at her partner, Lord Spencer's eyes were fixed on her hair, a flutter of light playing over his face as her crystal hairpin caught the sunlight. He did not look away for several seconds, her breath stuttering in her chest as she waited to see what he would do. After a moment, Lionel glanced about him warily and then tucked a loose strand of Charlotte's hair behind her ear.

It was a gesture that took seconds only, but the excitement and joy that burst through Charlotte's chest was something new. Lionel's hands returned to interlace behind his back, and they carried on their journey.

Charlotte's feet faltered as they went, Lionel's firm arm coming out to steady her.

***

Adam and Emilia reached the edge of the lake, looking out over the rolling hills of the English countryside. The snow presented a white patchwork winter quilt, and Adam exhaled happily.

"What a magical thing snow is," he said, "and tomorrow is Christmas Eve. I believe we will be blessed with a white Christmas."

Emilia stared out at the stillness and perfection of the landscape, her heart filled with a mixture of joy and disquiet.

"And after Christmas," Adam added, "I will be able to speak with your—"

"Lady Emilia!"

Emilia startled violently at the sound of Elderbridge approaching, her stomach in knots at the thought that he might have overheard them.

Have I spent too long with Lord Bellebrook? Has the duke come to comment upon it?

She turned with a forced smile as the duke skated up to them. He was still ungainly on his feet but seemed to have gathered some of his composure.

"Are you enjoying the skating?" he asked cheerfully.

Emilia was about to respond, but as the duke approached, it became clear he was less steady on his feet than she had first believed. It was obvious that he had misjudged his speed as he came up to them.

Emilia gave a startled shriek as he almost bowled her over. She was saved, however, by Lord Bellebrook colliding with the duke to stop him, the two men grappling with one another as they tried not to fall to the floor.

Emilia lurched forward and gripped the duke's arm, and finally, they were all able to right themselves.

"What the devil, Bentley!" the duke exclaimed. It was probably intended to be good-natured, but there was a sharp glint in his eye that Emilia was immediately wary of.

"My apologies, your Grace; I thought you were going to collide with us."

Emilia glanced at Adam. *What a diplomatic response,* she thought; *the duke would have barreled Adam into the bank if he had not stopped him.*

"Not at all, not at all," the duke said hurriedly clearing his throat loudly as he forcibly calmed his temper. The telltale sign of heat at his neck showed how angry he was but his lips curled all the same and he looked at Emilia with an expression that was almost fond.

"Will you accompany me, Lady Emilia?" the duke asked, holding out his arm.

Adam had the overwhelming urge to slap it away and even push the man to the ground for his audacity, but Emilia stepped forward and took it, and the duke sailed her away.

Emilia glanced back just at the last moment with a look of apology, and Adam watched them go with a spike of irritation so acute he felt like punching through the ice.

"Quite the pair, aren't they," Frederick said as he glided up to Adam, stopping expertly beside him in quite a contrast to the duke. Adam glanced at him, the irritation still bubbling beneath the surface, and nodded.

"They are indeed," *for all the wrong reasons.*

"I was trying to calculate the size of this lake compared to the one at your estate. Would you say it is about the same size or slightly smaller?" Frederick asked.

"A little smaller, perhaps. The rear pond increases its size beside the trout stream, I suppose."

"Ah yes, of course. Many happy times spent there, I do declare," Frederick said, his sharp features pink and shiny from the wind, his grey eyes almost exactly the shade of the sky above their heads. "It has been many years since we have skated on that lake; Anastasia would have loved this."

Adam ground his teeth, placing his hands behind his back and squeezing his fingers together.

Must the man mention Anastasia every time I see him? It cannot be an accident.

"She always wore the ice skates you bought for her that Christmas, do you remember? She spent hours dying the laces green, only for them to turn black eventually."

Adam remembered the incident well. It had been in the year when Anastasia had decided that absolutely every aspect of their house had to be linked to Christmas in some way. She had heard that it was possible to dye her bootlaces dark green from the white they had once been. She had spent hours leaving them to soak in the bowl, but then, when she had taken them out, they were completely black. She had had white skates and black laces for the rest of her life.

The rest of her life.

Adam cleared his throat, nodding to Frederick and followed Emilia and the Duke of Elderbridge at a safe distance, every strike across the ice a painful memory.

The joy of the day faded away to nothing as the sky darkened above his head.

CHAPTER NINETEEN

The evening brought the arrival of the Sternwood's grand Christmas ball.

It was more formal than the last, and many more guests were in attendance. Emilia's mother flitted about downstairs, instructing servants and complaining to the housekeeper about supplies that had not yet reached them.

Emilia and Charlotte got ready in her room. Charlotte had a serenity about her that Emilia was finding increasingly confusing. Usually, her friend was a bundle of nerves before a ball, but tonight she seemed utterly calm.

Emilia, on the other hand, felt sick. She knew that tonight was the final opportunity she would have with Adam to present their increased affection to the world. After Christmas, Lord Bellebrook would speak to her father, and it would have to seem as though they had a genuine affection for one another.

The unpleasant truth was that, despite their arrangement of convenience, Emilia was beginning to feel more for the earl than she had realised.

His kindness and sincerity upon the lake had undone her completely. She had been unable to get his words out of her head and often found herself musing on their life together as husband and wife. The thought worried her. She did not wish to be tied to a man who had only ever seen her as a convenient arrangement. She did not wish to get her heart broken.

"What is it, Emilia?" Charlotte asked, her brows lowering in the mirror.

Emilia stared at her friend, warring with herself about the best course of action. She did not know whether telling Charlotte what they had agreed to would betray Adam's trust, but one thing she was certain of was that Charlotte was her greatest supporter.

"Nothing," Emilia said quickly. "I am just aware that the duke is certain to ask me for a dance this evening, and I am anticipating his daughters' disapproval."

Charlotte did not laugh, her expression darkening. "Try as well as you can to stay away from the duke. A dance or two is inevitable, you are right, but if your card is continually marked by Lord Bellebrook, the duke will not have the opportunity."

Charlotte gave her a sidelong glance, and Emilia turned from her position in front of the full-length mirror to give her a warning glare.

"Do not pretend, Emilia, it does not suit you," Charlotte said, a hint of steel in her voice. "He has barely left your side all day today. When you fell on the ice on the way back from the village, I thought the connection between you both might melt the snow away altogether!"

Emilia could not help herself; she laughed loudly at her friend's phrasing.

Charlotte placed the final pin into her hair, pulling down a single strand to hang in front. She hoped Lord Spencer might repeat his actions at the lake and curl it behind her ear again. The sensation of it had been wickedly enjoyable, and Charlotte's heart was singing at the thought that he might make his intentions known tonight.

"And what about you?" Emilia asked archly. "Lord Spencer skated with you all day today and has made you laugh far too many times to be polite."

Charlotte gave her a fond smile. "He is amusing."

"Hah!" Emilia exclaimed in a most unladylike fashion. "We know plenty of *amusing* men; none of them have ever made you laugh as much as he."

The door opened abruptly, admitting her mother, who looked beautiful but harried, as she flapped her hands irritably at Emilia.

"Emilia! You are needed downstairs; will you stop dallying?"

But in the midst of her tirade, as Charlotte stood, Lady Sternwood paused, her eyes looking Emilia up and down with such approval that it rather startled her daughter.

"My dear, you look *very* well indeed. That gown is exquisite."

Emilia glanced at Charlotte, her brow lowering as she frowned in confusion. "Th-thank you, Mama," she replied.

Her mother approached her, smoothing a hand down the side of her dress and inspecting the fabric, holding it loosely between her thumb and forefinger.

"Thank you," Lady Sternwood said gently. Her eyes were wide and affectionate suddenly. "For all your support over the last few days. I feel that I have not been fair to you these last few years, and I am reminded what a wonderful daughter you are in times like this."

Emilia's heart clenched at the sincerity in her mother's gaze, for a moment it was just as it had always been between them—before the scandal had ripped them apart.

"I am looking forward to a brighter future for you with the duke," Lady Sternwood concluded, and the shining moment of joy died an infinite death. Emilia forced a smile.

"You're welcome, Mama."

Her mother placed a gentle kiss on her forehead and left the room. Before she had even closed the door, Charlotte's fingers were entangled with Emilia's, and the two women looked at one another in despair.

"That was a nice thing for her to say," Charlotte murmured.

"Yes. It's a shame she had to ruin it at the end."

"Come on. This ball will be a chance for some fun, at least. And it's Christmas Eve tomorrow. There is much for us to be cheerful about!"

Emilia could do nothing but laugh as her friend pulled her from the room.

***

They made their way down to the ballroom. More candles had been placed around the corners of the room, and the decorations were more heavily dominated by gold colouring and fabrics.

Her mother had instructed the guests to bring the 'season of Christmas' with their attendance, and there was a flurry of tartan, red, green, and gold about the room.

Many women had red feathers in their hair and beautiful gowns. Emilia had already worn her deep red gown and, therefore, had chosen gold tonight but with a dark green sash. She also had holly in her hair, which was much commented upon.

She stood amidst the milling crowds, listening to the rumble of voices all around her. She was frantic with excitement suddenly, Charlotte's reminder that Christmas Eve would be the next day had made her position all the more real.

After tomorrow, Lord Bellebrook will speak with Father, and everything will be settled. I just have to endure tonight and the next two days—then all will be well.

As if summoned by thought alone, it was at that moment that Lord Bellebrook was announced to the room.

Emilia turned, and the whole world faded away. Any illusions she had about their arrangement being only one of convenience also faded. Adam looked exquisite. Tall, stately, and every bit the earl he was, he was perfect in his strict black-and-white evening attire, and his cravat was intricate and flawless.

A tie pin at his neck sparkled in the candlelight. It was dark green, matching his waistcoat. Emilia swayed sideways as Charlotte nudged her pointedly.

"You're staring."

Emilia tried to drag her gaze away, but she was frozen in place by an invisible connection hanging in the air between them as Adam began scanning the crowds.

When his eyes alighted upon her, he walked immediately in her direction. Lionel walked behind him sporting a dark red waistcoat and looking very handsome indeed.

They were by far the most attractive men at the ball and walked through the crowd with many women looking their way as they did so. Having warned her friend not to stare, Charlotte could not take her eyes off Lord Spencer and was utterly speechless as he bowed, holding out his hand and leading her to the dancefloor without a word.

Emilia curtsied to Adam, who carefully ran his eyes over her figure and cleared his throat.

"You look very beautiful this evening," he said softly, and Emilia blushed up to her hairline.

"Thank you, my Lord," she said happily. "As do you."

Adam offered her his hand. "Will you do me the honour of the first dance?"

Despite her nerves, Emilia took his hand, her gaze furtive and flitting about the room as butterflies swirled in her stomach.

"Everyone is staring at us," she said with concern. Emilia had always known that they had planned and were orchestrating a deception but now the realities of it made her worry all the more.

"Try to focus on me," he said gently. "The fact that they are noticing us is a good thing. What has you so concerned tonight?'

"I suppose I did not think of what I was doing to my parents," she said as they took their positions on the floor. The rest of the dance floor was filled with people, the room a sea of faces, and Emilia swallowed around the lump in her throat. "I am not being honest with them."

Adam gripped her fingers tightly, his steady gaze meeting her own.

"My Lady... Emilia," he said hesitantly as Emilia's heart beat loudly in her chest. "You are not being dishonest. You are choosing the direction your life will move in. There is not yet an understanding between you and the duke. I will speak with your father in two days and make my intentions known. Try to focus on that. You have done nothing wrong."

Emilia was not certain she agreed with him, but she was grateful for his support and guidance. As the music began all around them, the band playing a lively seasonal tune that filled the room, they began the gentle pace of the dance.

Emilia sucked in a sharp breath as the dance continued. Emilia could feel Adam's eyes on her throughout.

Although he had instructed her to focus on him, it was as though she was unable to look anywhere else at that moment.

She would never have dreamt that their connection would feel so real to her in so short a time, but now it did. The fact that he understood how she felt about the duke, understood her scandal, and still wanted to spend the rest of his life with her was a seductive reality that she could no longer deny.

He was an eligible, impossibly handsome man who had made his interest in her clear. As Emilia watched him move about the floor with grace and experience, he was no longer the stranger she had met at the winter ball; he was her *betrothed*, and she was alarmed at how happy she felt in his presence.

The dance continued as they circled the room together, and by and by, there seemed to be no one else around them. Emilia felt lighter on her feet, her breath coming quicker in her chest as she looked into Adam's unwavering gaze.

Adam kept his back straight, his arms taut, trying to process all the emotions flooding through him as he held Emilia in his arms.

Even when he had courted Anastasia, he had never felt this intense need to protect and nurture someone. Just holding her against him was wonderful, a joy like nothing else flooding through him. He could feel the many eyes in the room upon them, but somehow, all he could see was her.

The hazel gaze he had grown to know so well punctured through his defences so that he felt raw and vulnerable again. Adam had promised himself long ago that he did not need another companion in his life, that he *could* not find someone else to love, and now all those certainties had been scattered to the winds in place of Emilia Sterling.

He stared into her eyes as they danced, the music blurring into nothing, the sounds around them fading. She felt *right* in his arms, and when he had called her Emilia, she had not blanched from him. The terrifying truth was that he could see a new path laid out ahead of him. Where before there had been nothing but empty, barren desert stretching as far as his eye could see, now there was a forest of colour ready for him to explore.

She has brought colour back into my world, which has been nothing but grey for years.

As the waltz ended, Adam and Emilia stood together for a fraction longer than the other couples, their gazes still locked as they slowly lowered their arms.

Adam's hand lingered on the small of her back for seconds only, but it felt like a lifetime to them both. It seemed that the pretence they had affected to convince the world of their affections was more than that now. Out of the ashes of their pasts, something real and true had begun to burn, too bright and fierce to deny.

Lionel and Charlotte were also standing at the edge of the floor, his fingers loosely brushing hers as they watched their friends gaze into each other's eyes.

Charlotte looked to Lord Spencer, who did not say a word, but his lips quirked as though with a secret he would not disclose. As she took his arm, the room seemed to vibrate with whispers as the couples walked back into the crowd.

***

As the ball came to an end, many guests began to gather in the drawing room. Before the carriages came to take those who had travelled to the ball home, a buzz of voices began to stir in anticipation of what was to come.

Emilia watched her mother pleadingly, but Lady Sternwood would not be dissuaded. She was insistent that her daughter would play the piano for everyone, no matter how many people were crammed into the tiny space.

It was by far the largest performance Emilia had done in several years and her shoulders were tense, her palms sweating as she took her seat at the pianoforte.

She knew Adam was in the crowd, could feel his gaze like a physical touch, and drew strength from it as best she could. Every time she sat before the piano, now, it was tinged with sadness and loss. She remembered Lord Julian's approach, the inevitable realization that she had overstepped, and the horror in the coming days of her reputation being systematically destroyed.

She placed her fingers delicately on the keys, took a deep breath, and tried to still her aching heart. Caroline and Penelope stood at the front of the crowd, watching her with expectant looks on their faces. It was as though they were anticipating her failure, and Emilia felt a strange certainty rush through her.

They do not know my talents and have no interest in learning them. I shall show them what talent truly is.

She began to play.

It was a pleasant Christmas tune, and she could feel the atmosphere in the room changing as she played it. Many were nodding their heads, and several of the older members of the crowd clasped their hands and smiled, as it was a well-worn tune she had heard since infancy.

With a jolt, she saw a man step forward out of the crowd. For a horrible, heart-stopping moment, she thought it was the Duke of Elderbridge coming to claim her in front of the world. But her heart leapt in her chest as she saw Adam come to stand beside her.

The room was absolutely silent around them beneath the notes of the piano, and Emilia continued to play, wondering what on earth he meant by this unusual display.

And then Lord Bellebrook began to sing the words that usually accompanied the music. Emilia was playing from memory, and he was singing from memory, too. His voice was beautiful, a melodic baritone that sailed through the room and over the heads of the crowd, exquisitely complementing the level of the music.

Emilia forced herself to remain calm, keeping her hands from shaking as best she could as his voice soared at the crescendo. In a moment of utter madness and delight, she began to sing the soprano along with him.

A single glance was all she needed. Adam looked down at her, and she looked up at him, and at that moment, all pretence fell away.

For Emilia, everything was suddenly very real, and she felt pure, undiluted happiness at the prospect of her future with this man. Not only had he come to support her while she played, but he could not have given a stronger indication of his affection for her than by doing so in front of so many people.

Emilia could have leapt into the air with the joy of it.

Adam continued to sing, the waves of the music coming back to him all at once. Lyrics he had not sung since childhood were somehow available to him again as though they had been locked away in a secret place in his mind, and only Emilia held the key.

He had not sung like this since Anastasia was alive, and it felt *right* to do it now. He was going to protect Emilia from the fate her parents had laid out for her, and he took great pleasure in doing so. She had looked so petite at the piano, almost afraid, but now they sang in harmony, their voices rising and mixing in the air, perfectly entwined just as it seemed they had always been.

He did not look at Emilia again, too afraid with so many eyes on them that his feelings would be plain for all to see before he had even confessed them to her.

They were together, *truly* together, in that moment, and he felt a smile spread across his face as he continued to sing. Someone in the crowd began to sing, too, and soon, the whole room was alive with voices, brought together by a union he had never expected from a woman he had come to care for in every possible way.

The song soared and wavered and lingered in the air and Adam knew that he would never forget that moment or this day for the rest of his life.

CHAPTER TWENTY

The following morning was Christmas Eve, and Adam woke early, his body feeling alive with excitement and fear.

The ball and the subsequent performance had passed in a blur, and he had had little time to accept or understand the feelings it had raised in him since he had come to bed. His head pounded with a heaviness that had nothing to do with the wine he had imbibed the night before.

He stood before the mirror, looking at his reflection, seeing the colour in his cheeks and the brightness in his eyes. It occurred to him that he looked like himself again. He examined his reflection and saw the man he once was, full of possibility and excitement, with a spark of life at his heels.

Even so, he still felt a bundle of nerves in the wake of all he had experienced. He seemed to waver between happiness at being able to be with Emilia and crushing guilt every time he thought of Anastasia. He was unable to reconcile all that had changed in so short a time. Only a month ago, if anyone had asked him if he would take a new wife, he would have denied it vehemently.

Now, he felt renewed at the prospect.

In an attempt to settle himself, he went to seek out Lionel, his cousin always acting as a steady rudder through any storm.

He wondered where Emilia was this morning, how she might be feeling—what she might be doing. *Emilia.* It was becoming increasingly difficult for him to think of her as 'Lady Emilia Sterling' now.

He walked swiftly through the grand hallway, which was positively bursting with Christmas cheer as the bowers and garlands hung heavy on all of the doorways.

Ahead of him, he saw the library and as he opened the door his shoulders sank back in relief at the sight of his friend sitting beside the window. The fire crackled pleasantly, the wind blowing outside, sending wafts of snowflakes past the window.

Lionel was engrossed in his book, and Adam noticed that he was on the final page, his eyes moving steadily over the page.

Adam waited patiently, leaving the door open, and approached softly, trying not to startle him. Lionel did not take long to finish the book, snapping it shut with a contented sigh and glancing up at him.

"Well, good morning," he said.

"How long have you been in here?" Adam asked with amusement.

"Several hours, I could not sleep and decided I simply had to finish this book before I spoke to Char—Miss Fairfax again."

Adam would have probed that comment a little more, but he had too much else on his mind to think of it.

Lionel's expression stiffened, and then a lazy smile spread over his face. "Did you wish to discuss something with me? Because I have been waiting for many days for you to broach the subject."

Adam frowned. "Am I so transparent?"

"Entirely. But then, you are the very best of men, and I am desperate to see you settled once more. Sometimes one wishes to see a thing when it is not a reality... but I hope that is not the case here."

"You had suspected?" Adam asked tentatively.

"I suspect many things. I would not be so arrogant as to assume I know your heart, especially with all that has happened in your past. But I have grown to hope..."

"You know I do not refer to Lord Cheswick's daughter?"

"Not unless you have become a halfwit without me knowing." Adam gave him a stern look, but Lionel shrugged. "I know it is not a gentlemanly thing to say, but every time the woman opens her mouth, I want to stopper it."

"Lionel!"

"It is true. Besides, I have a notion that you do not wish to discuss Lady Seraphina."

Adam scratched at his chin awkwardly. "No. Perhaps not."

"Lady Emilia is a marvellous creature; I could not be happier for you."

Adam stilled, looking into the fire and trying to make sense of all the emotions warring inside him. "I cannot understand how I have come to feel so strongly for her in such a short time."

"You have been living a half-life for years. Sometimes, when one allows oneself back into the world, emotions run in packs, like wolves."

Adam shrugged a shoulder, frowning into the flames.

"I loved Anastasia."

"Nobody in the whole world would deny it, my friend. I loved her, too. She was glorious." There was a long silence amidst the crackle of the fire, and Lionel laid a gentle hand on Adam's shoulder. "But she is gone. And you deserve to be happy."

Adam was aware of the tears banked at the back of his eyes now, but Lionel did not comment upon them.

"I have been so bewildered by these events and so surprised by them in equal measure. It has been far too short a time to really believe anything real could exist between us, but when we danced last night. The way she looked at me. I could hardly breathe."

"My dear fellow, are you becoming a romantic?"

Adam chuckled softly, grateful for Lionel's change in tone. It allowed him to gather himself and begin to pace before the fire.

"Every time I feel anything for Lady Emilia, I see Anastasia in my mind. I never believed I would want anyone else to share my life, but right from the beginning, when I first heard her play, there was a connection I couldn't deny. She touches something inside me that I do not believe even Anastaisa could penetrate. It is beyond understanding. It is beyond logic."

Adam ran a hand angrily through his hair as he turned back, feeling the warmth of the flames fading as he marched back toward the bookshelves.

"And you are sure this is a reality," Lionel asked evenly, "not a passing fancy? After all you have not been in company for a long while. Perhaps it is simply the closeness you have missed."

Adam stopped, staring at his cousin in disbelief. "Have you not been listening?" Adam asked, exasperated.

"Of course, but I am trying to help you," Lionel insisted. "You seem confused about how you feel; I am simply asking if it is real." Lionel shrugged a shoulder as though the idea was commonplace. "Perhaps it is merely proximity. This infatuation will fade in time, and then you can live your life as you had before."

The horror of that casual statement must have shown on his face.

"Of course it is real," Adam said forcefully. "Do you believe me so cold that I would simply lead a woman on like this without good reason? She has helped me to *feel* again. And this is something unique to her and her excellent character. Your mother dragged me to countless balls only a year after Ana died. I met dozens of women. *None* of them compare. Not even in the smallest way to what I feel for Emilia."

There was a ringing silence after that statement, and Adam felt anger and relief burst through him as he watched Lionel's face transform into a wide smile.

He had been tricked into confessing his feelings and without any subtlety whatsoever. Adam almost groaned at his own susceptibility.

"I believe we both know the truth now," Lionel said, smugness rolling from him in waves.

"You are a scoundrel."

Lionel chuckled, coming forward and wringing his hand before clapping him on the shoulder.

"Adam, you are like a brother to me. I have *longed* to see you begin your life again. And that is what you are doing. This is not *erasing* Anastasia it is celebrating her by allowing yourself to love for a second time. I believe, I truly believe, she would be happy for you. She would not wish for you to wither away into obscurity because of a lost memory. Be free, my friend. And tell Lady Emilia how you feel."

Behind Lionel amidst the shadows of the bookshelves, a dark figure stood in the faint glow of the firelight. Two eyes watching the men with mounting fury.

Frederick had been able to hear every word that the two men had exchanged, and he finally knew his time had run out. He was no longer in any doubt about the path he must follow. He could not allow Adam to confess his feelings to Emilia Sterling. And if her ultimate abandonment drove him back to his state of grief and despair then all the better.

All he had to do now was to convince the one man who could destroy their happiness to go along with his plan.

CHAPTER TWENTY-ONE

"You are in earnest?"

Emilia nodded, taking her friend's hands as Charlotte smiled happily back at her.

"We are engaged. He is going to speak to Papa. It might even be on the morrow that he does so, but I expect he will wait for Christmas to be over. I am sorry to have deceived you but I hardly could believe it myself. I kept thinking he would renege on it and tell me it was a mistake, but ..." The familiar fear threatened to overwhelm her, and Charlotte squeezed her hands.

"The way he looks at you cannot be mistaken."

Emilia pulled her down onto the bed as they sat beside one another. "And it would be my dearest wish to have you close, too."

Charlotte gave her an encouraging smile. "I would wish for that too, but nothing is certain."

"Lord Spencer has hardly spent any time with another member of the party," Emilia insisted.

"We are both dancing at the edge of true happiness, perhaps, but at least you have some certainty in your future," Charlotte said wistfully. "Lord Spencer has been most attentive, but he has not spoken of any *feeling*. He simply looks at me in a way that makes my heart sing."

"He will tell you. I have no doubt that he will," Emilia said. "He would not have spent so much time with you and under his mother's nose, no less, if he did not have intentions toward you. You make such a handsome and beautiful couple."

Charlotte's fingers tightened on her friend's, and she felt the weight of the last few years lift from her shoulders as she met her gaze.

"For so long, I wondered if you would be able to find happiness," she confessed. "I hate Henrietta Darcy for all of the pain she brought into your life, but perhaps sometimes these things happen for a reason. Without her, you would never have met Lord Bellebrook, and I would never have met Lord Spencer."

"Fate has a way of playing a hand when it is required," Emilia said, her eyes shining in a way that was new and infectious. Charlotte grinned.

"Two more days."

"Two more days, and then it will be Boxing Day, and Lord Bellebrook will speak to my father. I can only pray that Lord Spencer takes the initiative and does the same with yours. I will be the happiest woman alive to have us as part of the same family at last."

Charlotte had never seen her friend so forward in her desires or her excitement, and she felt a tendril of hope unfurl within her.

***

Frederick wandered through the house, nodding politely to the other guests and trying to keep his feet steady. He truly wished to run through every room and recover the duke immediately, but he could not afford to attract unwanted attention.

As he continued, he smelt the faint hint of tobacco on the air and aimed for it, knowing how much the duke enjoyed his cigars. Upon finding himself outside the parlour room, Frederick stopped, noting that the duke was inside but unwilling to approach him if he were with his daughters.

Frederick leaned as far as he could around the door, seeing to his satisfaction that the room was empty. The duke was sitting with his legs crossed in a low chair, reading the paper, smoke hovering above him like a cloud.

Frederick entered casually, trying to look as though he had not been seeking out the man for the last half hour. The duke nodded to him as he came within his line of sight, and Frederick returned it with a nod of his own.

"Would you object to me joining you, your Grace?" Frederick asked as calmly as possible.

The duke didn't speak, his eyes still on the paper in front of him, but pointed his cigar at the chair opposite, and Frederick sat down gratefully.

Where to begin... he thought, wondering how he might broach the topic without the duke becoming suspicious of his reasoning.

"Quite the storm," Frederick said, looking out of the window at the flurries of snow and the high wind. The trees were swaying alarmingly against a background of dark grey sky. The duke dropped one corner of the paper, seeming surprised by the view that greeted him.

"Good Lord, I had not noticed. This will be hellish to travel in; I am glad we are happily ensconced within these walls and will only have to make our way to church in the morning. At least it is a short enough walk."

He took a great pull of his cigar, and the smoke billowed out all about him. Frederick, who had never enjoyed smoking, held back the urge to cough, clearing his throat instead, and nodded at the duke.

"I have enjoyed this house party," he said patiently, biding his time. "Lady Sternwood always holds the best events, and I was sorry that they had not held one for a little time."

The duke's foot twitched. "Indeed. Well, all of that will be behind them soon enough."

"Of course, your Grace," Frederick said swiftly, leaping upon the topic, "I hear that you are close to securing Lady Emilia's hand. I can only congratulate you. It is an excellent match."

The duke glanced at him pompously, and Frederick deliberately moved his expression into a frown, furrowing his brows and sighing heavily.

"Is something amiss?" the duke asked.

"Oh no, nothing but the obvious. It will not be a problem after today, as you say."

The duke finally lowered his infernal paper and gave Frederick a long look. "The obvious?" he asked, his voice laced with suspicion, his own brows furrowing.

"I suppose it is inevitable that a woman so beautiful will have other suitors after all. And all of it will be forgotten by the time you propose."

He felt a thrill at the colour flooding to the duke's face. "Other suitors? What are you speaking of man?"

Is the man so obtuse? Frederick wondered. *So full of his own self-importance, he has utterly failed to see how much attention Adam has paid to Emilia. What a fool.*

"I did not mean to overstep, your Grace. I merely wished to congratulate you."

"What the devil do you mean, sir? Are you saying she has courted scandal once more? That there is some impropriety here?"

"No. Nothing of that nature. Merely that I have noticed Lord Bellebrook showing her some attention. I suppose it is harmless enough."

To Frederick's dismay, the duke seemed to dismiss the idea, shaking his head.

"Adam Bentley has no designs upon anyone. He is in mourning. Flouncing about in grief for all the world to see. It's pathetic."

Frederick was surprised that the duke spoke so openly to him—he was *also* a Bentley, after all, but the duke seemed to be a man who believed that his wealth and status protected him from most things. Whatever the reason, Frederick was glad to be brought into his confidence.

"I only thought it odd, that is all," he mused, speaking more slowly.

The duke sighed. "Thought what was odd?"

"The length of time they were together on the lake. Almost the entire morning, skating together and he had his arm around her waist." That finally got the duke's attention. "And then... at the piano last night, they seemed close. I thought it might have concerned you." The duke sat forward in his chair, and Frederick took the chance to trivialise his own comments. "I am sorry to have troubled you with it. Clearly, I misunderstood."

Frederick pretended to get up and stopped immediately when the duke held out a hand, halting him, his eyes sharp and calculating.

"His hand about her *waist*?"

"Indeed, your Grace. Lady Emilia would never be so foolish as to court scandal, but sometimes a lady cannot prevent a man from overstepping his bounds."

The duke rose slowly to his feet, throwing the paper behind him as Frederick waited for the inevitable explosion with suppressed relish.

"That is not to be born. I have an understanding with her father. I was with my daughters for much of the day; I confess I did not see what you described. But I thank you for bringing it to my attention."

"Of course, your Grace," Frederick said sweetly. There was a pause that was a little too long for Frederick's liking as the duke contemplated the carpet beneath his feet, his cigar forgotten between his fingers. "Might I suggest, your Grace, that if you have an understanding with Lord Sternwood, you act upon it forthwith? It is not my place, and I would never presume to tell you how to act, but there have been some comments and gossip over the last few days that have led me to believe it is not only myself that has noticed Lord Bellebrook's attention."

The duke's eyes flashed at that, and he took another long pull of his cigar, blowing the smoke carelessly about him and right into Frederick's face. It took everything in him not to choke on it.

One more hint, and I think I have him.

"I would not wish to see the great name of Easton courting scandal. If you were engaged to the lady, I am sure this would be cleared up instantly."

The duke finally stiffened and nodded, stubbing the cigar out on a table behind him and turning back to face Frederick with a look of purpose that the other man welcomed above all things.

"As I say, you have my thanks," the duke growled. "I had not realised it had reached such a degree. I knew that Bentley had been paired with her a few times over the past week, but I was not under the illusion he had any designs on the woman. She is going to be *my* wife. Her father has promised her to me. That shall not be put asunder."

"I am glad to hear it, your Grace."

"Indeed." The duke eyed him for a moment, a long look that put Frederick's teeth on edge, but after a long pause, he gave him a curt nod and left the room.

Frederick watched the duke retreating back, stopping himself from jumping for joy at the success of his plan.

One more push and Adam will lose everything he ever wanted, and that title will be mine.

CHAPTER TWENTY-TWO

Sternwood Manor buzzed with excitement. The lighting of the Yule Log was the final event before Christmas Day, and everyone was in very high spirits.

Many of the guests were laughing together in the great hall, waiting for Lady Sternwood to arrive to light the log. The hubbub of many voices and the odd shriek of laughter echoed around the corridors as servants flitted about making the final arrangements before it took place.

Emilia and Charlotte came downstairs together, their eyes bright with excitement on the eve of a day that might change their futures forever.

Emilia's footsteps were soft upon the marble stairs, and she linked her arm in Charlotte's as they approached the guests, who were chattering happily in small groups. The Cheswicks were speaking to the Pinkertons on the edge of the room, and Seraphina was the only member of the party who seemed visibly out of sorts.

Emilia felt a pang of guilt at the downcast expression on her face, aware that any rumours about the growing connection between herself and the Earl of Bellebrook would have doused Seraphina's hopes for a match in that quarter.

Emilia's guilt grew as she was unable to suppress the vicious wave of satisfaction she felt at the knowledge.

As they reached the final steps, Emilia saw Lord Spencer look around, his eyes alighting on Charlotte. If Emilia had entertained any doubts of his feelings for her friend, they were gone instantly with that look. Even Lady Spencer looked delighted to see Charlotte, and it was clear everyone involved approved of the match.

Emilia's heart swelled for her friend. She was eager to go over to the Spencers immediately, but before she could do so, her plan was thwarted by a footman who approached her to request that she make her way to the drawing room.

Emilia frowned at him in confusion but could not deny the request.

Leaving Charlotte in the capable hands of Lord Spencer, who gallantly came forward to join her, Emilia went to the drawing room, feeling an inexplicable sense of unease wash over her the closer she came to the door.

She pushed it open find her parents standing in the centre of the room, quite alone.

She frowned, the sense of unease growing as she took in her mother's ecstatic expression and the stoic happiness on her father's face.

"My darling girl," her mother said, walking toward her, her skirts sweeping behind her as she took her daughter's hands. "I am so proud of you. I could weep."

Emilia stared at her, glancing over her mother's shoulder to look at her father.

"I always knew things would come good," Lord Sternwood said happily. There was an air of confidence about him that Emilia had not seen for many years; it sent a chill down her spine. "Finally, I am able to release you to the capable hands of a good man who can secure your future."

Emilia stared at him, dumbfounded.

"Benedict Easton, the Duke of Elderbridge, has come to see me this afternoon," her father continued. "He was most eloquent in his manner and bearing and has asked for your hand in marriage. I can tell you without hesitation that I was happy to accept it. I am thrilled and beyond proud of the connection that you have secured." Emilia's heart plummeted to the floor. "I would never have expected such a match and am thrilled that it has come to pass after everything you have been through."

She looked at her mother, and the tears shining in Lady Sternwood's eyes made Emilia's stomach turn over.

"To think, the Sternwood name will now be linked with the Elderbridges." Lady Sternwood sighed as though all of her dreams had come true at once. "I know this will be a transition for you, my love," she said earnestly. "There will be obstacles in your future that you will overcome. But I have no doubt this will be the beginning of a great step forward for you. What a wonderful match. What a glorious Christmas present for us all."

Emilia was aware she was standing mutely with her mouth wide open. Unable to retain her strength any longer, she sank slowly into the chair behind her, unable to think of a single intelligible thing to say. Her mother smiled at her warmly, taking her silence for shock and happiness.

"We will go and light the log, just as I had always planned, but this year, it marks the beginning of a new life for us all."

Lady Sternwood clapped her hands in delight as she reached out to her husband. Lord Sternwood crossed the room to join his wife, and they stood together, waiting for Emilia to do the same.

Although Emilia felt as though she might faint at any moment, she could not muster the strength to ask her parents for a reprieve. This should have been the happiest time of her life—for her parents, it was.

With feet of clay, she stood, forcing a smile to match their joy, and followed them slowly from the room. She wondered why she could walk so steadily on a floor tilting on its axis. Why could she put one foot in front of another when a great chasm had opened beneath her, ready to swallow her away from this world and into oblivion?

Everything is over now. I cannot refuse the duke. My father has given him his blessing. If only I had foreseen this. If only Adam had not waited.

They walked as a family into the great hall, the high ceilings dancing in the candlelight. A myriad of fabrics met Emilia's gaze, a swirling array of purples, reds, and greens as the women and men walked about, waiting for the event that would mark the true beginning of Christmas.

Emilia stumbled a little, drawing away from her parents and seeking refuge within the crowd around her. Thankfully, most of the people present were too enthralled by what was to come to analyse her behaviour too closely.

Four footmen had gathered at the doorway to the room behind the guests. The log itself was magnificent, twice as long as the year before and three times as thick. The men carrying it were already breathing hard, and as her mother swept before them, there were many exclamations as the log was carried forward toward the hearth.

Emilia sank further into the crowd, not wanting to catch Charlotte's eye. Her friend was standing beside Lord Spencer, only inches separating them. For the briefest moment, Emilia felt no happiness for them, only pure, unbridled sorrow and jealousy.

As she stood silently staring after her parents, a servant passed by and handed her a glass of sherry. It took everything in Emilia's power not to drink it in one gulp. She felt as though she might swoon; her head dizzy, the blood pounding in her ears, and each sound in the room was loud and alarming, as though magnified to five times its normal volume.

Her mother had reached the hearth, and the whole room was admiring the log against a background of excited chatter.

The log had a wide circumference and a large section at the front that twisted outward and almost split it in two. When she had first looked upon it, Emilia had been excited for when it was lit. Now, she looked upon its gnarled surface, and the wood was no longer magnificent; it was twisted and scarred—beastly and ugly to her eyes.

The crowd stood in rapturous silence as Lord and Lady Sternwood came to stand beside the log as it was placed before the fire on a special brace fashioned for the purpose.

"Ladies and gentlemen," her mother called out. "With this log, we honour the spirit of the season and the warmth of home and hearth. May its flame burn bright and bring light to the darkest days. We ask for health, happiness, and prosperity to all within these walls, and may its warmth bless our friends and family near and far."

Emilia's eyes sought out Adam in the semi-darkness. Like all the others, he was watching her parents, but now and again, his gaze would move about the room as though searching for something. Emilia sank further into the crowd, horrified at the thought of him seeing her now. He would never be able to look at her with kindness and understanding again.

"As we kindle this fire," her mother continued, carrying a taper toward the log as the footmen lifted it and placed it into the hearth itself. "May it carry away the troubles of the past and guide us with hope into the new year. To peace, joy, and good fortune for all."

Lady Sternwood sprinkled the log with salt, which cracked and popped in the nearby flames, and Lord Sternwood poured whisky over the top. The resulting flame along its length was blue in colour and violent at first, as the crowd went wild with applause as the log was lit and everyone toasted the event.

Emilia drank her sherry in one gulp now, her fingers flexing so firmly against the stem of the glass that she thought she might break it.

Peace, joy, and good fortune will never be in my future. I shall never be happy again.

Adam watched the bright orange flames illuminate the enraptured faces before the hearth. He looked about the crowd, eager to find Emilia and toast the lighting of the log with her. Lady Sternwood's words had filled him with renewed hope and gratitude for the life he was to begin with her. He could not wait to celebrate by her side.

Turning, he finally spied her at the back of the room. She looked terribly pale, and he felt a jolt in his gut at the sight of her expression. Frowning, he moved slowly between the guests toward her, eager to ascertain the reason for her unhappiness and to do all he could to make her smile again.

However, before he could, there was another stirring in the crowd, and Elderbridge stepped forward in front of Lord and Lady Sternwood, his glass raised.

Adam paused, not wishing to appear rude by continuing to make his way through the guests in so small a group and waited for the duke to make his toast before returning to Emilia.

"My lords, ladies and gentlemen," the duke shouted over the hubbub of voices, and everyone fell silent again. For a long moment, there was only the sharp crackle of the log behind them and the quiet clink of glasses as the servants moved about the room.

"I have another announcement to make," the duke said with a smile, his glass still raised. "I would like to make a second toast. The first, I will repeat, for it was of an excellent and worthy nature and should be celebrated with the joy of the season behind it." Everyone raised their glasses with him and Adam began to move, but it was clear the duke was not finished yet.

"Indeed," Benedict Easton rumbled on, "Lady Sternwood's words filled me with much greater joy than any other in this room. The depth of my own happiness lies with this family, after all." He looked around him, a smug smile curling his features as he sniffed and raised his glass for a second time. "I would like to announce the news that I am engaged to Lady Emilia Sterling and could not be happier to celebrate with you all tonight on this most auspicious occasion."

With that, the duke turned, his eyes searching the crowd just as Adam had done. He lifted a hand, and, like a ghost moving through the room, Emilia emerged and walked toward him. Her expression was impossible to read, utterly blank and devoid of feeling.

At the front of the room, her parents watched on with fond smiles. Lord Sternwood raised his glass, and the room all toasted the happy couple.

Adam stood stock still as the crowd began to applaud. The sights and sounds around him faded into a muted blur. He stood in a vacuum of nothingness, numb and utterly broken.

On the edge of his hearing, he thought he heard the faint chime of a pianoforte, a lively tune that splintered into being and was then cut off abruptly on a discordant note, the sound ebbing away, as though it had never been there at all.

CHAPTER TWENTY-THREE

Emilia held her glass aloft like an automaton, forcing a smile onto her lips and keeping her eyes above the heads of the crowd. She could not bear to meet Adam's gaze.

"To the happy couple," the crowd chanted, and glasses chimed around the room.

Emilia was not spared from seeing the reactions of the duke's daughters, however, no matter how much she tried to avert her gaze. Their presence was like a dark shadow in the corner of the room, eating away at the merriment of the rest of the group.

The three girls were positioned at the front and to the side of the hearth. As the yule log burned ever more brightly and Lord and Lady Sternwood accepted many offers of congratulations, the duke's daughters stood silently like statues, watching their father in apparent disgust.

Sophia was better at hiding her feelings than the others. Penelope looked revolted but was attempting to smile. Caroline was tearful, and Emilia could see her holding her older sister's hand.

Sophia's bright blue eyes, so like her father's, met Emilia's, and the hate and anger in them almost made her step back to hide behind the duke's large body.

She ripped her gaze away, not wanting to see the unhappiness in his daughter's eyes match her own. But as soon as she did so, her gaze alighted instead on the one pair of eyes she had dreaded. In the centre of the crowd, standing still as stone, was Adam Bentley. The usually soft and warm expression on his face was a mixture of horror and fury. Emilia's heart lurched at the sight of it, and everything came crashing down.

There were voices all around her: whispers, sighs, and high, shrill laughs that cut through her brain like glass. She could not focus on anything, the blood pounding violently and loudly in her ears. She fought to keep herself upright, but there was blackness at the edge of her vision.

She imagined Adam striding forward, a mask over his face, his eyes cold and angry as he looked down at her as though she were nothing. Adam would look at her with pity and loathing and he walked from the room, never to be seen again. The thought was a fresh lance of pain through her chest.

Her mother's smiling face was on the edge of her vision, and Emilia knew, above everything else, she must uphold her honour. She could not be seen to let her mother down now. As far as her parents knew, their wildest hopes had just been made a reality. She could not let them down. Not again.

Emilia staggered to the side, her hand loosening from the duke's grip. Elderbridge turned to her, his broad smile fading as he frowned. Slowly, the smile on his lips faded to a snarl of irritation as she felt herself stagger sideways again.

She had never swooned in her life, but with the emptiness in her mind, she knew that must be what was happening. Blackness was edging into the sides of her vision. It was as though time stood still, her own body moving as though through molasses, a syrupy slowness to her movements as she watched her hands flail wildly into the air in a wide arc.

She fell backwards into the oblivion that had finally come to claim her. The thought of it now was a welcome one. She longed to sink into the darkness of the world, to be lost to it where no one could find her and be at peace, away from the suffocating pain of losing Adam forever.

There were shouts and cries of dismay on the edge of her hearing as she felt her hip jar against the floor just before her head hit the cold surface. The pain was staggeringly sharp, and she sighed, trying to right herself and stand up again, but it was no use. She fell back, the coldness of the floor seeping into her skin as she lay helplessly on the ground.

The last thing she remembered was a shape above her and a hand cradling her head. Somewhere nearby there was a frantic voice, sheer panic in every syllable as it called for a physician. It sounded like the Earl of Bellebrook, but she knew that could not be the case.

Adam will never look at me again.

At the sight of her friend's distress, Charlotte shoved her way through the guests, careless of the unhappy looks she received from those she removed from her path.

Emilia's crumpled form hit the floor just as Charlotte reached the front of the hall, and she darted forward as a familiar and welcome presence arrived at her side. Lord Spencer strode forward, all authoritative composure, clearing a path for her to get to Emilia's prone form.

Charlotte hurried forward, kneeling at Emilia's side. She risked a glance upward at the duke, but he had already turned away and was speaking in a low voice to Lord Sternwood. Charlotte could have kicked him for his arrogant, disinterested expression.

Charlotte turned away, rage coursing through her veins at the man's audacity. If she could have dragged Emilia away from this place and never allowed her to set eyes on the duke again, she would have done it in a heartbeat.

In the next instant, Lord Bellebrook was kneeling beside her, leaning over Emilia.

In comparison to the duke, Adam's face was ashen pale. His eyes searched Emilia's face, and his hands fluttered over her as though unsure whether to touch her.

"We should get her to her room," Charlotte said decisively as Lord and Lady Sternwood came forward, both of them frowning and looking genuinely concerned.

Charlotte bore them no ill will for what they expected of their daughter, but she was not going to sit by and allow them to give the duke authority over what happened to her friend. He was just the type of man who would command a room, and Charlotte did not believe he had any place in deciding what was in Emilia's best interests.

"Send for a physician," Charlotte said, about to say that a footman could carry Emilia to her room, but her voice died in her throat as Adam gallantly lifted Emilia from the floor.

Adam's expression brooked no argument, and with a brief nod to Lord Sternwood, he carried her from the room with Charlotte and his cousin in his wake.

They left the duke standing uselessly in the great hall, a grimace on his face as he watched Lord Bellebrook's retreating back. He made no attempt to help his future wife, glaring after them all as though they had orchestrated the whole affair.

Adam carried Emilia's limp body up the stairs, his heart pounding, his lungs straining at the panic that threatened to consume him. He was grateful for Lionel, who was a steady force at his side, striding up the stairs and opening a door ahead of him.

Adam only registered it must be Emilia's bedroom when Miss Fairfax followed him inside as he laid Emilia gently down upon the bed. She was still deathly pale, but he could see her chest rising and falling gently.

A heavy hand on his shoulder made him jump, but as he turned, he saw Lionel's concerned face as his cousin nodded toward the door.

"We should leave the ladies to it. A physician has been summoned," Lionel said gently, and Adam allowed himself to be led from the room. He knew he could not linger, yet his mind and body screamed at him never to leave her side.

He looked back at her prone form and felt the same all-encompassing fear as he had felt by his mother's side and then by Anastasia's. He would not sit idly by while another woman he loved was ripped away from him.

As the door closed behind the two men, Charlotte pushed some hair from Emilia's forehead, squeezing her hand and stroking her cheek.

"Emilia?" she whispered. "Emilia, darling? It is Charlotte. I am here."

She took hold of Emilia's hand, but it was cold and clammy. Charlotte looked at the clock on the wall. It was late in the evening, and she only hoped that the doctor would be able to reach them soon. It was Christmas Eve, yet all of the season's joy had been snuffed out. She sat utterly still, watching Emilia's face as the snow fell past the window, wondering what would become of them all now their world had fallen apart around them.

***

As Lionel and Adam reached the bottom of the stairs, Adam could hear the hubbub of many voices from the great hall and was grateful when Lionel swiftly led him into the quiet of the library. He did not have the strength to answer any questions just now.

The door snapped shut behind him as Lionel took some of Adam's weight and pushed his cousin into a chair, walking to a small drinks cabinet in the corner of the room and pouring them both a large glass of brandy.

He returned to Adam, handing him the glass, which the other man took, staring at the amber liquid inside it as though he had never seen such a thing before. His eyes were glazed and unseeing. It was so horribly reminiscent of when Anastasia had died that Lionel felt a jolt of fear in his heart.

Could Adam take this kind of pain again? Could he come back from another loss? He simply did not know.

"She will be alright," Lionel said decisively, wishing too that he could have stayed with Charlotte to comfort her. She had looked pale and frightened, and he had hated to see it.

All he wanted to do was take her into his arms and tell her everything would be alright. Lionel was more determined than ever to express his intentions now. If he had not had to support his cousin, he would have marched straight up to Lord Fairfax and asked for her hand right at the moment.

"What can it mean?" Adam's voice was a whisper. "She told me she hated him. She told me she did not wish to marry him. She accepted my *hand*! What is happening?"

Lionel sat opposite him as they both took a long swallow from their glasses.

"It must be a mistake," Lionel stated quickly, voicing what he had felt in his heart as soon as the duke had made the announcement. "Emilia's reaction is not one of a woman who is excited at the prospect of marriage. You said her parents approved the match? Perhaps this is their doing, and she has had little or no say in it. It would not be the first time."

"She is betrothed to me," said Adam, not hearing him. "She told me she would accept me; she danced with me… I felt… I cannot…"

Lionel leaned forward squeezing Adam's hand none too gently.

"Listen to me," he said firmly. "We will get to the bottom of this."

Adam stared at him, swallowing around the evident emotion he was trying to conceal.

"I do not deserve happiness. Perhaps this is what I get for—"

"No!" Lionel said, almost shouted it and Adam jolted in his chair. "We will not speak of such superstitions. There must be an explanation, and I will find the cause."

The two men sat together, nursing their drinks, Adam not speaking at all. Lionel watched his cousin with a heavy heart, wondering what on earth could have led to this disaster.

In the great hall, the guests were still murmuring about Emilia's health. The duke had retreated to a large window, waiting to hear news from Lord and Lady Sternwood, and was being largely ignored and allowed to be alone following the collapse of his betrothed.

Lord and Lady Fairfax were muttering together in a corner while the Marchioness and Countess spoke urgently to their daughter across the room.

Frederick stood beside the yule log, watching the merry flames dance over its surface with joy in his heart and a discreet smile on his lips. He glanced at his mother, who was asleep in a chair on the other side of the room, and then returned his gaze to the flames.

He held a glass of port in his hand. The servants had all dispersed to seek physicians and see to the family, so there was a considerable lack of service. He had almost drained his glass, but there was just enough left to raise it silently to himself and toast his good health.

Things could not have gone more perfectly, he thought cheerfully. *It is only a matter of time now. I am sure that Adam will not be able to take this fresh blow.*

Now, it was just a case of securing *his* future. He glanced up at the duke's back, outlined against the falling snow pattering against the black window before him, and finished his port with a single swallow.

CHAPTER TWENTY-FOUR

Emilia's head was pounding.

She woke to the sound of birdsong and a shaft of light across her pillow. The fire was crackling, the world outside a sea of white.

It was Christmas Day, and she felt wretched.

"Emilia?"

Charlotte was at her bedside in moments, gently placing a cool cloth over her forehead. Her gaze was all concern, and there were dark circles beneath her eyes—she looked as though she had not slept at all.

Emilia frowned at her, trying to fathom why she felt so terrible and why she was in her bed. She thought back to the night before and everything began to unravel in her mind. She remembered the Duke of Elderbridge stepping forward, the smug arrogance on his face as he claimed her in front of everyone.

She could only imagine what Adam had thought. He must believe she had deceived him all this time, that she had never intended for their proposal to be real. Yet again, he had been abandoned by a woman in his life. The thought that he might believe she had chosen a duke over an earl to elevate her status after the scandal flitted through her head.

She groaned.

"Are you in pain?" Charlotte took her hand, squeezing it gently as she watched her.

"What happened? Why am I here?" she asked, dreading the answer but desperate to know.

"You fainted and have not regained consciousness since. The physician has been and will return shortly with your draft."

"I fainted?" Emilia asked in disbelief. "I have never fainted."

"I think it understandable given the circumstances. I cannot believe the duke announced it in front of everyone. Is it true?"

Emilia winced as she nodded her head. "My father and mother called me into the drawing room just before the ceremony. They were so happy, Charlotte and I could not speak. I did not believe he would do it. Not yet. I thought... I thought..." she trailed off.

"Lord Bellebrook carried you here," Charlotte said softly. "He wouldn't allow anyone else near you; he just lifted you up as though you weighed nothing at all."

Emilia's heart beat more rapidly at that knowledge, but she sighed, a heavy weight resting on her chest.

"He must despise me," she lamented.

"I do not believe that is the case."

"How could it not be? He must believe I lied all this time, that I was never intending to marry him. He has seen such loss in his life, and now I am only compounding it."

She sat up, determined to go and find Adam and explain her side of the story, if nothing else, but a gentle hand pressed her back to the bed.

"My love, you must rest," Charlotte said, standing again and repositioning the towel that had fallen against the pillow. "Nothing is certain, and Lord Bellebrook is a rational man. He will know what the duke is."

"And what can he do? What can anyone do now?"

"Do not lose faith. You are stronger than this. You must regain your strength and face the world as we all must." Emilia looked back up to Charlotte, startled by the vehemence in the other woman's voice. "*You* have not accepted the duke. Your parents may wish for the match, but they cannot force your hand."

Emilia attempted a brave smile, and Charlotte seemed mollified, but she knew it was not so simple. It would break her mother's heart if she refused now, and she could not see a path ahead of her where she would be able to live the life she had dreamed of.

This is a most dismal Christmas, indeed.

***

Everyone had gathered in the parlour room to wish each other joy.

But despite the brightness of the room and the merry garlands all around them, the company was a sombre group.

Adam had been touched by the obvious concern of so many. Lord and Lady Fairfax had asked if there was anything they could do and had summoned the family physician who lived close by to tend to Emilia.

Lord and Lady Pinkerton had been suggesting different tinctures that he might employ to alleviate Emilia's symptoms.

Adam's mind was stuck on one image in a cycle: Emilia's crumpled form. Her lovely face against the cold marble, her body limp in his arms.

He sipped his mulled wine, staring out of the window, trying to ensure that his face did not betray his inner turmoil. He wanted to be alone in his study in the silent company of books and wished he had never come to this damned house.

Just like that, the thought solidified in his mind. *I must leave.*

He knew that Elderbridge would be crowing about his betrothal as soon as Emilia was well again—or perhaps even sooner if he knew the duke as he believed he did. Adam gulped down the last of his wine and walked slowly from the room, not wishing to attract any unnecessary attention.

He found a footman in the hall and instructed him to prepare his carriage. Walking up the stairs to his room, he staunchly avoided looking at Emilia's bedchamber door and made his way to this room.

Villiers looked startled as he entered. The man had been cleaning his shaving brushes and looked up in consternation as his master re-entered the room. He hastily put down his things and stood.

"My Lord, my apologies. What can I do for you?"

"Pack my things, Villiers, please. I will be leaving this morning."

Adam knew it was damnably unfair to his faithful valet to make him travel on Christmas Day of all days, but he could not bear to remain for a moment longer.

Before he could instruct any further action, however, the door opened, and his aunt burst into the room. In the way of quiet authority she always had, she waved Villers back as the valet bowed to her. He retreated into a side room to pack Adam's things, and Adam watched his aunt close the door, looking at him with an expression of stoic determination.

"What are you doing?" she asked.

"I am leaving. What does it look like?" Adam said with a clipped tone he knew would rile her instantly. His aunt scoffed loudly as he walked to his bedside, picked up his book, and began to pack the travelling case stored beneath the bed.

"You are running away, you mean?" his aunt asked, and Adam paused, glancing up at her. She was tense, her stare unmoving, distant, and fierce.

"I am *leaving*," he said with more anger than he had thought he possessed.

"It is Christmas, Adam," she implored, her expression softening as he rummaged through the room. "This is a time for family. Please. Stay for the day. You do not know what has—"

"I was a fool to open my heart again. I know that now. I was mistaken about Lady Emilia, and I will pay the price for it."

"Do you truly believe that girl knew what the duke would announce?"

"She accepted him, did she not?" Adam spat, the fury coming to the surface so fast he felt like hurling something through the window.

"You are being a fool," his aunt returned, taking a step toward him. "You will honestly leave without speaking with her?"

"And what should I say? Everything is already settled."

Augusta laid a gentle hand on his arm. "I do not believe she would treat you this way."

"You do not know her," Adam said, throwing her off and walking to the middle of the room, looking about helplessly for something to occupy him.

"But *you* do," his aunt insisted, and Adam closed his eyes. "Do you believe this is how she would conduct herself?"

"It does not matter," Adam said bitterly. "She has made her choice."

He continued packing, his aunt a silent force by the bedside, but she said no more. Adam would not be reasoned with and was determined to leave as soon as possible.

He would put Sternwood Manor and all the happiness he had felt within its walls behind him, and he would *not* look back.

***

Lionel walked through the ground-floor corridors in a daze. There was a strange stillness across the house, as though the very walls were holding their breaths. It was the strangest Christmas he had ever experienced, and his heart ached for his friend.

If he had not been certain that his actions would have broken his cousin even further Lionel would already have approached Lord Fairfax to ask for Charlotte's hand in marriage.

Seeing her caring nature had only doubled his feelings for her. Knowing she had sat beside Emilia's bed all night, he had been unable to sleep, wishing he could go to her and show her some comfort.

Lost in thought, he continued down a side corridor, but his pace slowed as voices drifted toward him through the air. There would have been nothing remarkable in that except that they were the only jovial voices he had heard all day.

Suddenly aware of a door ajar ahead of him, Lionel felt the need to silence his footsteps as he moved closer, instinctively knowing that he was overhearing something private that he should not have been privy to.

"It is true; I have long believed we could make a great alliance."

That was the duke's voice. Lionel moved closer to the crack in the door.

"The Bellebrook estate has been mismanaged for many years." Lionel froze as he heard Frederick's voice. "My cousin is weak. When his late wife passed, he had fits so strong he was bedridden for weeks. He will not be able to survive another blow, I am sure of it. It is only a matter of time before I am named as heir, and then the names of Elderbridge and Bellebrook will be synonymous with one another."

Lionel peered around the door, noting that both men held cigars in their hands and glasses of whisky. They clinked their glasses together.

"I am grateful to you for pointing out their attachment," the duke said. "I had intended to secure the marriage in the New Year, but knowing Bentley's preferences allowed me to see clearly how I should act."

"It would have been an imprudent match. Emilia is young and foolish; her head may have been turned by my cousin, but it will not stay so now. She will provide you with the heir you need and secure your line. That is what matters, your Grace, and I would not have wished to see the chance slip by you."

"Indeed, I am in your debt."

"I had not expected the lady to fall ill, however." *Was that a hint of regret in Frederick's voice?*

"She will survive. Women always like to make a show of things to have the required effect, but she will come to heel when I tell her. She knows her duty, as does her father. She's a timid thing, I have always thought so, scared of her own shadow. My preference would always have been to align myself to an untainted family—the Sternwood name is hardly the exalted position I would wish for the Elderbridges, but my options are limited."

Lionel clenched his fists, his breathing laboured as he considered what he had just heard. He thought of Adam's ashen face the night before and the alarm and pain in Emilia's as the announcement had been made. He was now certain that Emilia had known nothing of what had occurred—this was a deal between gentlemen just as he had suspected. Lord Sternwood would have agreed with the match outside his daughter's wishes.

Lionel was furious.

He had never felt so angry or so betrayed, and by *Frederick* of all people. Lionel knew the chequered history that Adam had with the man. Frederick had always considered himself the victim in everything, believing that Adam should have given him more of his fortune when his father died. As it was, Adam had gifted Frederick with almost five thousand pounds only two years before, and the man had frittered it all away in gambling hells all over London.

Lionel moved closer to the door, considering bursting into the room and accusing them in the midst of their heartless celebrations. But he stopped himself, taking a gentle step back. *This is not my fight.*

He had to find Adam.

As silently as he could, he turned back the way he had come and walked swiftly to the main part of the house, leaping up the stairs two at a time in his search for his cousin.

He burst through the door of Adam's room to find Villiers carrying a trunk as though to head down to the carriage. Adam, dejected and pale, stood behind him with a black bag in one hand. He frowned at Lionel as he entered, concern flitting over his face.

"Is it Emilia?" he asked, moving to place the bag on the floor. Lionel's hope surged; if his cousin was still concerned for her well-being, he had not allowed his disappointment to eclipse everything else just yet.

"Villiers, could you give us a moment?" Lionel asked respectfully. The faithful man lowered the trunk and left the room, closing the door with a smart click.

"What is it, Lionel?" Adam asked, his voice weary.

"There are games a foot, just as I thought." Lionel stepped forward, fixing Adam with a long stare. "Frederick is behind this."

Adam scoffed. "Of what are you speaking? He has forced the duke to propose, is that it?"

"He warned him." Adam's cynical smile died on his lips. "He must have discovered that you were betrothed to Lady Emilia in secret and told the duke so that he would propose before you had the chance to make it official."

Adam stilled. "How do you know this?"

"I just heard them congratulating one another. Frederick spoke of you in terms so abhorrent I can hardly believe the man is of sound mind. He appears to believe that one more disappointment will have you withering away and leaving the estate to him as he has always wanted. At which point it appears he will align himself with the duke. Much good may it do him when he would have squandered your father's fortune in months."

Adam took an urgent step forward. "You are sure of this?"

"I heard the duke thanking Frederick for informing him of your intentions. Frederick must have overheard some of your conversations with Emilia or learned it some other way, but the reason for the hasty betrothal was to ensure you could not be aligned with her. It is all a plot by Frederick to get your title and align himself with a powerful man. The only thing the duke wants from this marriage is a male heir, he said that he would 'bring Emilia Sterling to heel'."

At those words, Adam's expression changed, and for the first time in three years, Lionel saw the man who had been lost to him.

The grim determination on Adam's face was all-consuming, and he marched from the room, nodding his head at Lionel for him to follow.

CHAPTER TWENTY-FIVE

The two men walked beside one another down the stairs, and without a word, they headed toward the billiard room. The stillness over everything felt just the same, but now the air was charged with tension.

Lionel jerked back in shock as Adam slammed his foot into the door of the billiard room, all the fight and the drive that had been missing returning to him in an instant.

Frederick, who was alone at the billiard table, still smoking his cigar with a second glass of whisky at his elbow, jumped back three feet and stared in wild confusion at Adam.

Adam could feel the energy pulsing through him. He was flooded with guilt once more, but this time none of it was for Anastasia—it was all for Emilia.

How could I have dismissed her? How could I have doubted her so entirely? I am a blaggard and a fool, and I will do everything in my power to make it up to her for the rest of my life.

"As you can see, Fred, I am still living," he spat, bolstered by Lionel's reassuring presence at his elbow. "Or had you hoped that I might have expired even in the few moments since you manipulated the duke's hand into ruining me?"

Frederick's mouth was hanging open like a fish. He stared at Adam, his gaze flicking between him and Lionel. Then, there was the sound of running footsteps, and Lord Sternwood loped into view, pausing as he took in the scene with a raised eyebrow.

Frederick backed away from the table, dropping the cue from his fingers and staring around like a caged animal.

"What the devil are you talking about?" he asked, but his voice was thin, his face pale.

"I am speaking of the conversation that Lord Spencer just heard between yourself and the duke. Do you deny it?"

Lord Sternwood came to stand beside Adam, his eyes sharp but wary.

"What... I have not..." Frederick asked. His gaze was flitting about the room frantically as though looking for an escape.

"I heard you," Lionel said, his voice a dark promise of retribution. "You were congratulating one another on a job well done. You have manipulated the duke into securing his match with Lady Emilia Sterling in haste because you do not want Adam to remarry. You have been after his title for years, and believed another loss would destroy him."

"No, I—" Frederick was spluttering wildly.

"I am told you think me weak," Adam said. "I remember when Anastasia died, you were at the house almost daily, pretending to be sorry for my condition, when I knew in my heart you were there merely to rejoice in my decline."

Frederick stuttered but could find no words to reply.

"My Lord," Adam said, turning to Lord Sternwood. "The duke and my cousin have been conspiring to use your daughter as a pawn in their scheme. Mr Frederick wished to thwart my *honourable* intentions towards your daughter so that he could ally himself with the Elderbridge name."

"What is the meaning of this?"

The duke entered the room, looking like a carbon copy of Frederick at that moment. They could not have done more to confirm they were in cahoots, smoking the same cigars, drinking from the same glasses. Adam could not have planned it better if he tried.

"Do you deny it?" Adam demanded, feeling a wave of satisfaction that he could finally speak down to this odious man.

"Deny what?" Benedict roared, but as his gaze fell on Frederick, he paled.

"You brought forward your proposal after my cousin warned you that I had intentions of my own. You care nothing for the lady in question, only for your own future."

Lord Sternwood was staring at Adam in consternation.

"Of what is he speaking?" Lord Sternwood asked, staring at Adam in bewilderment as Lionel stepped forward, pointing a finger at the duke.

"The Duke of Elderbridge and Mr Frederick were discussing their alliance. The duke spoke of your daughter as though she were a dog he could bring to heel. What was it you said?" Lionel asked, turning to the duke with suppressed fury. "That you would prefer a family that was 'untainted' but that your options were limited. The Sternwoods, after all, are far from the *exalted status* of the Elderbridges."

Adam turned to the duke. The man was gaping at Lionel in horror, and Lord Sternwood, who until that point had been a mask of confusion, turned to him, his face mottled with red blotches of anger.

"I *beg* your pardon, Duke; what did you say of my family?"

The duke shook his head. "I did not mean—"

"You called my daughter *tainted?*" he stepped forward, rage pulsing from him in waves. "I have spoken to you at length of her disgrace. You were one of the few voices of reason. You even knew the Blackmoors and are on intimate terms with Lord Julian. You *knew* she had done nothing, behaved exactly as she should. That was the only reason I allowed you anywhere near her."

Adam was taken aback by Emilia's father's passion. He presented himself as rather withdrawn, only wishing to secure Emilia a good marriage, as many fathers did. But the person standing before him now was vibrating with indignation, his eyes sparking with fury as he glared at the duke.

"I will take the degradation of our alliance out of your hands, *your Grace,*" Thomas Sterling snarled. "If you wish to find yourself a woman who is *untainted*, you can find her in the halls of the society you so bitterly crave."

The duke stuttered a blustering apology, but Lord Sternwood would not hear it, turning his back on the man in disgust. After a moment of paralysis, the duke retreated from the room, the cigar falling from his fingers as he did so.

Adam turned to confront Frederick for a second time, but the man had escaped through the rear doors while they were distracted by the duke, and Lionel swore loudly and set off in pursuit of him. That left Adam alone with Thomas Sterling, who was still puce with anger, but his expression sharpened as he looked back at Adam.

Adam bowed.

"My Lord, I have not been entirely honest with you myself," Adam said quickly. "I suppose you may wonder about my involvement—why I would care about the duke's intentions for your daughter."

"I would," Lord Sternwood said slowly, "if I had not witnessed you together over the last few days."

The astute expression on the man's face made Adam hesitate and as Lord Sternwood's shoulders relaxed Adam straightened his own, determined to begin to make amends—starting here.

"My Lord, I love your daughter," he said earnestly. "It is not something I ever expected to happen, but it is true. From the first moment I stepped into this house, I knew that my life was going to change forever. She is everything to me, and I have been a fool to doubt her. I believe I can make her happy. I ask you most solemnly for her hand in marriage. I will spend my life trying to deserve her."

Thomas Sterling's face was a picture of surprise and amazement, but eventually, he smiled, his eyes twinkling.

"The duke was not what I wanted for Emilia, not in himself, but I wanted to secure her future. I have had many sleepless nights since the scandal about how she will live. Elderbridge presented a decent option but I will not deny I am glad she is free of him." Thomas gave Adam a long stare, and he fought to hold it. "You are a good man, my Lord. I have seen as much with the way you treat those around you and the friends you keep. I would be honoured to align the name of Bellebrook with Sternwood—but I will not make the same mistake twice. If Emilia agrees, you have my blessing, not before."

Adam shook his hand, and just as he did so, they both heard the distant sound of a pianoforte. Adam's spine stiffened at the familiar notes, and Lord Sternwood smiled.

"That can be only one member of my household," he breathed a sigh of relief. "Go to her. I believe you have a question for my daughter."

Adam walked out of the room as quickly as he could, a strange echo of the first afternoon he had spent in the house overcoming him. He had not known when he walked down this very corridor that his life would change forever.

He waited outside the room, listening to the familiar notes playing, and closed his eyes, letting them wash over him for a moment.

Slipping inside, he watched Emilia's fingers move across the keys. The tune was mournful and sad, and her expression was the same. Adam was desperate to make her smile again, deeply ashamed of himself for having assumed the worst of her.

"Emilia," he said softly, and she snatched her fingers from the keys, turning to him. There were shadows beneath her eyes, and her cheeks were blotched with tears.

He walked up to her quickly and lowered to his knees beside the piano stool. She drew in a sharp breath, staring down at him in amazement as he dared to take her hands in his and stared up at her, trying to convey in a single look all the love and sorrow he felt.

"Lord Bellebrook," she said, her eyes looking to the door behind him, trying to tug her hand free from his grip.

"Adam," he replied, and her gaze fell on his once more. "I would prefer you to call me Adam."

"I cannot!" she said, trying to pull her hands free again as fresh tears began to fall. "

"Emilia, listen to me; it is all over." She frowned down at him, letting out a long breath. "My cousin Frederick told the duke of my intentions toward you, no doubt having observed us together in recent days. He used that information to force the duke's hand to thwart any chance of me remarrying. He has always been desperate to inherit my fortune, and if I married again, his chance of that would be gone forever."

"But my father—" she said helplessly.

"Lord Spencer overheard them speaking of you. The duke was callous in his description, calling you tainted following the scandal. Your father heard of it and has called off the engagement."

Emilia stood up, swayed on her feet, and sat down again, staring down at him in astonishment. The rush of pure relief that she felt was almost overwhelming and she clasped Adam's hands more tightly.

"He has called off the engagement to the duke?" she asked, her voice small and desperate.

"He has." Adam hesitated as his fingers tightened around her own. "I can only hope that I am not too late. That you can forgive me."

"Forgive you?" she asked. "What could I need to forgive you for?"

"I was blinded by my jealousy and anger, Emilia. I thought you had betrayed me, lied to me. My own demons had a hold of me. I should never have doubted you. I am sorry." He took a deep breath. "And most of all, I wanted to tell you that I love you."

Emilia's eyes were shining with tears now, and as he stood, she did too. They stood together in front of the window where the snow had begun to fall again.

"You have lit up my life—your music, your wit, your intelligence. I came here dreading everything I would have to go through, and now I am happier than I can say that I took that leap. I will do everything in my power to deserve your love and nurture it for the rest of our days if you will have me."

Emilia wiped at her eyes, the bright brilliance of his words shining through her like a shaft of sunshine. She had never felt such all-encompassing joy, and she smiled.

"When you first proposed to me on the terrace, I felt something had been growing between us since the beginning, but I was too afraid to name it. We have both been hurt in our lives, and we have both experienced loss. Over the last few days, I began to feel something far more than I ever thought possible. There is nothing to forgive, my Lord—"

"Adam."

"Adam," she said with a shy smile. "I am so grateful that we found each other."

"As am I."

"I love you," Emilia said softly as he took another step toward her. "I cannot wait to share my life with you."

Adam lowered his head over hers and finally claimed her lips with his own. They stood together as one being, their lips moving against one another, their arms coming around their bodies as they held each other close.

Outside, the winter wind rippled through the snowflakes on the bright Christmas Day, and a ray of sunlight pierced through the clouds illuminating the world around them in bright, perfect light.

EPILOGUE

One year later...

Emilia moved through the corridors of Bellebrook Manor, looking about her at the decorations and Christmas colours on every surface.

Her mother had arrived a few days before, and they had spent many happy hours ensuring the manor was exactly as it needed to be for her first holiday as the countess of Bellebrook.

As she tweaked with a ribbon on the back of one of the chairs, a low chuckle sounded behind her, and she turned to see Adam leaning against a doorway, watching her with a soft expression.

"It is quite straight, I assure you. Everything looks perfect."

She arched a brow at him, but he simply laughed. "I am merely ensuring I do not disgrace you," she said with mock irritation as he came toward her and took her into his arms.

Bending down to give her a long kiss, he pulled away, smiling at her cheerfully.

"Is that what you are in danger of doing?" he asked. "And all this time, I believed it was *I* who might disgrace *you*."

She hit him playfully on the chest, taking his hand and pulling him toward the drawing room where the rumble of voices could be heard. They had a variety of guests staying with them this holiday season. After the success of her mother's party the year before, Emilia had insisted that Bellebrook Manor would be the location for the next Christmas.

The intervening year had been the most wonderful of her life. She and Adam's feelings had only grown stronger and brighter since their confessions on Christmas Day, and everything about their time together had been beyond perfect.

Emilia still laughed at the memory of her first day visiting Bellebrook Manor before the wedding had taken place. Adam had been so nervous that she'd had to reassure him that nothing about a *house* could dissuade her from marrying him. He had spoken of placing a pianoforte in every room, much to her amusement, and even after many months together, it was still his favourite pastime to listen to her while she practised.

As they entered the drawing room, Adam grinned at Lionel, who stood by the window looking at his wife with consternation. Charlotte was holding something up for him to try, and Lionel leaned away from her in disgust.

"But they are honeyed chestnuts, dearest," Charlotte was saying. "You surely cannot *dislike* them."

Charlotte placed a nut in Lionel's mouth, and he grimaced, making Emilia laugh heartily at them both as her friend shrugged and took a handful for herself.

"I do not understand him," Charlotte said as she noticed Emilia in the doorway. "They are just delicious."

Lionel had proposed to Charlotte as soon as he heard Adam and Emilia's happy news, and the two couples had been nearly inseparable for the past year. Emilia and Charlotte spent as much time as they could together, and if they were not at each other's sides, they were writing letters between their homes.

Bellebrook Manor had also changed beyond recognition with Emilia's influence. To Adam's surprise, she had never begrudged him the time he needed to spend on matters of the estate. She had understood very quickly that he would always have business to attend to—but it was the room he worked in that she objected to.

Only two months after they were married, Emilia had transferred everything from the library into his study and vice versa. He had her to thank for his beautiful study, looking out over the ground of his estate with long, high windows that let in light from every angle. His aunt had commented more than once on how gloomy the old space had seemed, and Emilia would smile fondly at her, giving Adam a knowing smile.

"Are you alright, my love?" Emilia asked, pulling Adam from his thoughts and he kissed her hand gently, putting an arm over her shoulders.

"I am quite alright, thank you. I had just realised I had not wished you a merry Christmas."

Emilia laughed. "You did this morning. Three times!"

He kissed her all the same, and she grinned up at him as he pulled back. "Merry Christmas."

"Merry Christmas, my Lord," she said mischievously.

"Will you have a roasted chestnut?" Charlotte asked, holding the bowl under his nose. "I cannot understand why Lionel will not have one."

"The same reason Adam does not eat fruit cake," Emilia complained as Adam took a handful of nuts to placate Lady Spencer.

Adam looked over at Lionel who was leaning against the counterpane with a weary smile, his eyes fixed on Charlotte, as they often were when she was in the room. Adam had never seen him so at peace, and they had spoken often over the intervening year about how much their lives had changed for the better.

Anastasia was still a part of Adam's past and always would be, but any guilt he had harboured about his love for Emilia had long since disappeared. Emilia asked him about Anastasia often and insisted on keeping her memory alive, even in his new life with her. It had helped him move past his feelings of pain and guilt and remember the happier, more wonderful sides of his old life with her, even as he basked in the new.

They all made their way to the front of the room where Lord and Lady Sternwood were speaking to Charlotte's parents as Augusta sat in her armchair sipping a cup of tea.

The fire was crackling fiercely in the grate and keeping the bite of cold from the room, even as the snow continued to fall outside in great sheets.

Emilia chuckled as Adam took her hand and dragged her over to the pianoforte.

"Everyone is demanding carols," he said blithely, placing a hand on her back as she settled into her seat.

"Everyone?" she asked with a smile.

"Can you not hear their clamouring?" he asked.

"I believe they are all rather distracted my love, are you sure you do not simply wish to sing?"

"Whatever makes you say so?" he asked cheerfully, but she took her seat as she always did and smiled up at him as she began to play a Christmas tune.

It was not long before the whole room was singing, their guests gathered around the piano, candles sending flickering light about the room bedecked with holly and ivy on every surface.

Emilia sighed happily as Adam's hand came to rest on her shoulder, and their voices rose in harmony, ringing through the halls of the home they had built together.

As her fingers moved effortlessly over the keys, she thought of all that had passed between them in the last year.

Frederick had been exiled from any decent society after his conduct at the Sternwood's house party, his debts and his reputation finally catching up to him. It did not help that the duke quickly distanced himself from Frederick in all respects.

There were many rumours of his fate and several reliable sources had said that he had fled with his mother to a remote family estate where he was living out his days quite alone, avoiding the bailiffs.

Emilia looked up at her mother's smiling face as her parents joined in the chorus and felt a rush of contentment at the sight. Over the past few months, they had grown closer again, Adam and Lady Sternwood had grown very close over the past year with the absence of his own mother.

Camilla Sterling had confessed that she had not understood Emilia's true feelings toward the duke, insisting that if she had told her, she would never have forced them together. Emilia had accepted it, even if she found it hard to believe. Her mother would always be a social climber and had greatly enjoyed her return to society over the last season.

Lady Seraphina Cheswick was now Lady DeGore and had married very well. Her husband barely spoke at all but seemed content to listen to his wife chatter endlessly to everyone in his vicinity. Emilia rather suspected it was a love match and was happy that there had been a positive consequence to their tumultuous year.

As the carol ended, the whole room erupted in applause, and Emilia chuckled when Adam remained at her side.

"I believe they wish for more, my love," he said firmly.

"I will play for as long as they will listen," she replied.

"I could stand beside you forever like this," Adam said softly. "I may never allow you to rise from that stool."

He leaned down swiftly and captured her lips in a brief kiss right in front of everyone in the room, and Emilia blushed fiercely. Adam's hand moved briefly to her rounded belly, where the promise of new life to come completed their Christmas picture.

Charlotte and Lionel came to stand beside them, and they all joined in a rousing chorus as the fire crackled merrily and the snow glittered at the window.

EXTENDED EPILOGUE

The manor echoed with the sound of excited laughter as Adam knelt beside his daughter.

"Come *on*, Papa," she said, her little hands twisting in his coat as he pushed the stem of the holly into the buttonhole on her dress.

"Darling, are you certain you want to have holly against you all day? What if you should prick a finger?"

"I will be careful, Papa," she said as the final push secured the stem, and she twirled before him. Her bright blonde ringlets bounced around her head, and Adam smiled down at her, his chest tight with affection. In spite of her five-year-old brothers, Melony had the entire household wrapped around her little finger. She had a talent for getting her way.

"Do you like my dress?" she asked, holding out her skirt for him to inspect.

"You look like a Christmas angel, my darling. Just like your mama."

"Did I hear my name?"

Adam turned, his smile broadening as Emilia walked into the room. She had on a gown of dark green and looked absolutely stunning, as always.

"I was just saying that Melony looks like an angel," Adam replied ruefully, and Emilia gave him a knowing look. Of all the people in the household, Adam was the most susceptible to Melony's charms. He put it down to her being so like her mother. He longed to make her happy and indulged her every whim.

"You are as bad as Augusta," Emilia scolded, picking up Melony, who squealed in delight as her mother spun her around as they made their way toward the parlour where their guests were assembled.

"Where are the boys?" Adam asked.

"They are both being showered with gifts. We are going to have the most spoiled children in society if we are not careful," Emilia said with a long-suffering sigh, but Adam wasn't fooled. He knew how much she loved the influence of her parents on the children.

As they stepped into the parlour room, the scents of pine and cinnamon wafted over them and Adam took in a long breath. It had been many years since Christmas had brought him anything but joy and seeing everyone gathered around the fire only deepened his excitement at the season.

It was Christmas Day, and his aunt had been staying with them for almost a week. She adored their boys, Michael and John, and played with them all day if she had enough stamina. Three other children sat before the fire, playing with some wooden toys. Elizabeth, Tom, and Grace Spencer were regular visitors to the house. Augusta adored them all.

Charlotte sat beside Lionel on the settee, watching the children playing.

Tom turned from his position by the fire, seeing Melony being lowered to the ground by her mother and gravitated toward her instantly. Much to the amusement of everyone present it seemed they were a love match as babies. They could hardly be separated from one another and Emilia and Charlotte often joked about their wedding day.

Adam sat beside Emilia as Augusta stepped forward alongside Thomas Sterling.

All of the children stilled in their play as Augusta looked down on them all. She had the perfect blend of stern and loving, and even Melony behaved herself when she was about.

"Who has been good this year?" Augusta asked. Thomas Sterling chuckled as Michael and John both raised their hands enthusiastically. "Have you indeed?" August asked, looking at Lord Sternwood in surprise. "Should we give them their presents, my Lord?"

"Oh, I should think so," Lord Sternwood said happily as Melony wrapped her arms around his legs, and he lifted her up for a kiss. "I think they've waited long enough."

Camilla Sterling chuckled from her chair beside the fire as there were squeals of delight all about them. Charlotte's parents were a little further back from the rest of the group, watching the proceedings with quiet enjoyment. They had always been more reserved than the Sterlings around their grandchildren but loved them to the same degree.

Michael trotted up to his father, proudly holding out the wooden soldier that Augusta had bought him. Adam shot his aunt a warning glare, knowing how expensive it must have been, but his aunt averted her gaze, and he could only smile.

"It is most beautiful. Have you named him?" he asked.

"I am going to call him Benedict," Michael said innocently, and Charlotte almost choked on her mulled wine.

Adam's gut clenched at the memory of that name, but it eased immediately as his wife's hand came to rest on his arm.

"It is a fine name, after all," she said evenly. "And I have not heard it, *nor thought of it*, for nearly five years."

Adam leaned back on the settee, putting an arm around his wife. The spectre of Benedict Easton had not troubled them for many years. He had married the younger daughter of a baron who was eager to make her way in the world, and by all accounts, they were content. Adam could only surmise that his daughters would never be happy with anything and was relieved that he no longer had to entertain them in society. They had all married and moved away outside of London, and they rarely saw or heard of the Eastons these days.

Emilia nestled into his side as he squeezed her shoulders and looked down at her.

"I have not thought of him," she murmured. "I suppose he is living his life somewhere."

"I imagine he is," Adam said, his jaw clenching. "I do not wish to think of him. I could not stand the man at the best of times."

"That is because you were falling in love with me," she replied, and he rested his head against hers with a long sigh.

"Right from the start, I think. The moment I saw you at the piano, I was lost; I just did not know it."

"I remember seeing you watching me and wondering what you might be thinking. You were such a handsome devil."

Adam chuckled. "Were?"

"Oh, are you expecting compliments, my love?"

"I am. Always. I have such a beautiful wife; I wish to match her."

"There is no doubt about that," Emilia said cheerfully. They both laughed together as the children began to clamour for carols around the piano.

It had become one of Emilia's favourite traditions to sit at the piano on Christmas day and sing with her family. It reminded her of everything she had lost and all she had gained with her life alongside Adam.

She was so happy with her lot in life, and things were made even better with Charlotte and Lionel in the mix. Even as she thought of them,

Lionel came to stand beside her, smiling down fondly at her as Charlotte sat beside her on the stool.

Emilia chuckled as Charlotte began to play the simplest melody she could remember; one they had played as children.

"Is this a duet?"

"It is," Lionel said sternly. "Bentley get over here, would you? We need to sing for the ladies. Thomas. Come and join us."

Lord Sternwood approached behind them, and Emilia began to play the easiest tune she could think of, much to Charlotte's amusement. Everyone laughed through their singing at the myriads of missed notes and the children all shouted to be let in on the joke.

Adam laid his hand around Emilia's shoulders as she continued to play, both of them remembering how different their lives had been many Christmases ago when an arrangement of convenience had blossomed into a rich and wonderful life filled with love.

It was a beautiful scene, a family around a piano, singing carols on Christmas day. Bunches of holly were tied at the window, and the bright red berries were a cheerful reminder of the season.

As their voices raised in chorus within the cosy room, a robin hopped onto the windowsill, pecking at the stone beneath and fluttering away into the snowy landscape.

~ The End ~

Printed by Amazon Italia Logistica S.r.l.
Torrazza Piemonte (TO), Italy